ONE TOUCH

Visit us at www.boldstrokesbooks.com

By the Author

Three Days

One Touch

ONE TOUCH

by

L.T. Marie

2012

ISBN 10: 1-60282-750-8
ISBN 13: 978-1-60282-750-9

This Trade Paperback Original Is Published By
Bold Strokes Books, Inc.
P.O. Box 249
Valley Falls, NY 12185

First Edition: October 2012

CREDITS
EDITORS: VICTORIA OLDHAM AND SHELLEY THRASHER
PRODUCTION DESIGN: SUSAN RAMUNDO
COVER DESIGN BY SHERI (GRAPHICARTIST2020@HOTMAIL.COM)

Acknowledgments

There are a lot of moving parts in developing a story, and I would like to thank all who have helped me in the process.

First, to my editor, Victoria Oldham. You truly make the editing process enjoyable. Thanks for keeping me on track and making sure all my i's are dotted and t's are crossed.

To Shelley Thrasher for tightening my story. Your insight is invaluable.

Sheri, it's truly amazing how your artwork captures the essence of the story. Once again, fabulous job!

To our Alpha leader, Rad. What can I say? This cub is proud to be a part of your pack.

To Tina, my wife, partner, and best friend. I look forward to all our adventures together no matter where they may lead us.

And last but not least, I want to thank you, the reader, for picking up my books and reading my stories. Without your encouragement, messages on Facebook, and all the e-mails I receive wanting more, the writing process wouldn't be as rewarding. You all rock!!

Dedication

To Tina,
My traveling partner. My lover. My friend.
Ti amo

Chapter One

"Flynn, touch me."

"I already told you I can't do that, darling."

"Yes, you can." Natasha placed Flynn's hand firmly between her legs. "See, I'm so ready for you, baby."

Flynn wasn't surprised to find the evidence of Natasha's need pulsing against her fingertips. There'd been a time when she wouldn't have been able to refuse such a blatant advance. This wasn't it. "That's a tempting offer. But my answer is still no."

Natasha pulled away, her expression incredulous. "You're serious?"

"As a heart attack."

"But…I don't understand."

Flynn gazed out over the horizon, taking in its majestic beauty. The journeys that had once fulfilled her had finally left her at a crossroads. The next step was uncertain, but she was convinced that treading old ground wouldn't help her find her way.

"I know you don't. But then again, neither do I."

"That makes two of us," Jaime Rivers said, with a final tap on the keyboard. Angry that her train of thought had come to an abrupt halt—again—she shoved her chair away from the desk. The problem was always the same. A few sentences, then nothing. "Shit, Flynn. What path? Choose already so I can get this damn manuscript written!"

The blinking cursor taunted her. It beckoned to her, saying, "Finish your thought, finish your thought." What a concept that would be after months of struggling. But hey, she'd finally managed a few lines. Now the question was, were they worth keeping or should she highlight the entire scene and hit Delete?

Battling with Flynn's character had tested Jaime's mental strength. The direction of this final chapter in her popular romantic series would mark the end of Flynn Russell's adventures. It would be hard to imagine a day without thinking up a new exploit for Flynn. Flynn's character had brought her comfort and strength during many lonely hours, but the time had come for Flynn to choose a path in life. Apparently, she wasn't the only one.

Flynn was exciting to write about because she was everything Jaime wasn't. Flynn hungered for adventure. She could operate anything from an airplane to a submarine and had the ability to attract women with a glance. Flynn was untouchable, unflappable. She could get out of any situation, but she couldn't settle down with one woman. That fact alone had kept *The Quest* series from ending, and five years later, Jaime had already published three books in the series. Her Web site received thousands of e-mails from fans thirsting for more. But the last year proved uneventful and still the words wouldn't come.

A writer without words was like breathing in a vacuum. She was suffocating, drowning in her own desolation. When the words vanished, they'd taken Jaime's passion with them. Writing wasn't fun anymore. Sentences no longer flowed from her like they used to, freely and easily.

Back then a few pain meds were a prerequisite to writing. They dulled the pain long enough to fuel her creative juices, kept word after word flowing like molten lava through her veins. The drugs masked the pain long enough to increase her productivity, giving her the ability to be whoever she wanted to be. And so, through her stories, she chose to be Flynn Russell, lesbian lothario and lead character in her award-winning lesbian adventure series. Surprisingly, while her body was numb, everything else became clearer. *The Quest* series was born in a wash of chemicals.

Giving up the pain meds had killed her creativity, left her with nothing to alleviate the pain and nothing to keep the words flowing. Only when she could block everything out did she feel the most inspired, the most alive.

It had taken time to recuperate from her near-death experience, but dreaming up Flynn's character made her feel whole again. She loved thinking about Flynn and her many exploits. Women always wanted to warm Flynn's bed, but when they awoke the next morning that bed was empty and Flynn was gone, off on her next adventure. As time progressed, though, Jaime began to sense a change in her character. Maybe it was time for the series to end. Maybe Flynn was ready to settle down. But with who?

"Hell. If I knew that maybe I could get my editor off my back and write the last book," she muttered.

It would be so easy to go back to the way things used to be. One pill could ease all her suffering. But that would make her a failure, and she'd learned the hard way from her mistakes and vowed never to visit that dark place again. Usually she could count on over-the-counter medications to help, at least until a muscle spasm hit—a jarring reminder that acetaminophen would never be strong enough.

The coffee pot's buzzer signaled her morning pick-me-up was ready. Caffeine was her only indulgence lately, which unfortunately did nothing to distract her from thinking about the pain or help spur her imagination.

As she reached for the coffee carafe, she pitched forward and hissed in pain. Bracing herself on the breakfast counter, she tried to breathe through the cramps that spread like hot needles through her abdomen. Aftershocks sent wave after wave of rippling spasms through her ribcage, finally bringing her to her knees. The phone rang and she glared at it.

Who the hell would be calling her at this hour? It couldn't be her dad, who was God knows where since his status in the military meant that most of the time his whereabouts were secret. That left her editor or her pesky best friend. She'd already had a lengthy conversation with her editor at five in the morning about the lack of a new manuscript. That left one alternative.

"What!" She held the phone in a death grip, still trying to catch her breath.

"'Bout damn time. What the hell took you so long?" Darlene asked.

"Sorry." She grimaced as the spasms tapered off. "You interrupted my all-night sex romp."

"Oh, you're hilarious. I know that's not it, because if you had anyone over they wouldn't be there after sunrise. Seriously, though. You okay?"

Darlene had her pegged. Sex was fine and very one-sided. No sleepovers. No exceptions. "Stop being a worrywart. I'm fine."

Darlene was not only her best friend but the only person who truly knew of her daily struggle. Darlene had found her in a pool of her own vomit the night she overdosed on pain meds, and since then Jaime had to constantly reassure her. Darlene had coaxed her into rehab and was the one person in her life she could trust not to betray her confidences.

"I can hear the pain in your voice. You had a spasm, didn't you?"

"Okay, fine. I had a spasm but it stopped. By the way, do you know what time it is?"

"Yep, sure do—got a watch, thanks. I called to see if you have plans today."

"Nope, and I'd like to keep it that way." She wasn't in the mood for company, as usual. Darlene had been on her for weeks to get out of the house yet still she refused.

"Humph, just what I thought. Sorry, pal. You're going to have to rearrange your busy schedule. I'll be by in ten minutes. You've been dodging me long enough about this reunion cruise."

Damn. She shouldn't have answered the phone. How many times did she have to tell Darlene that no way in hell was she getting on that oversized tugboat? When the brochures had arrived in the mail, she hadn't had to read past the raised gold letters proclaiming "reunion" and "cruise" to know she wasn't going to participate. High school wasn't worth reliving, and she couldn't imagine spending an hour with her graduating class, let alone an entire week trapped with them on a boat. She'd been treated like an outcast the entire four years and really only had one person back then she could call a friend. High school was ancient history and would stay where it belonged, in the past.

"Hello? Jaime? You still there?"

"Yeah, yeah, unfortunately. You know, today's not a good day. Maybe we can get together sometime next week."

"Nice try. You're going to look at this stuff and we're going to register today. My hubby doesn't want to go so we can be roomies for the week."

She looked out her kitchen window and sighed. Why couldn't Darlene understand that she didn't want to relive the supposed "glory days"? She couldn't find anything glorious about those memories, which in some ways were more painful than the injuries she'd sustained during her accident. "Please. Don't push me on this. I've already told you. I don't want to go."

"Yes, I know what you *said* but I know what you *need*. You can't keep hiding from everyone. Part of your recovery is to be able to adjust to the real world. My job as your friend is to help you achieve that goal whether you like it or not."

"But what if I'm not ready to meet the world?"

"No worries. That's why you have me. I'll introduce you. Now, do you need anything before I get there?"

"No, but thanks." She gingerly rubbed her side. "I promise. I'm good."

"Okay, pal. See you in a few."

Dropping the cordless phone onto the couch, she spent the next few minutes removing the newspapers and empty coffee cups that cluttered her living room. True, Darlene was her best friend, but sometimes she acted more like her mother than her friend. She loved Darlene and would do anything for her, but Darlene should understand better than anyone why she didn't want to take a trip down memory lane.

The scent of freshly brewed coffee followed her as she trudged down the hallway to answer the door, feeling like an inmate taking her last walk down death row.

"Hey," she said as Darlene pulled her into a hug.

"Hey, yourself. Feeling better?" Darlene asked.

"I told you I was fine."

"I'd believe it if you didn't look like someone shot your dog."

"That's impossible. I don't have a dog."

"Smart-ass," Darlene said, giving her a quick peck on the cheek. "So much for me trying to be nice."

"Nice…you? Let me guess. Body snatchers?"

"You're such the comic today. Besides, that's so fifties. I was thinking more *Aliens*."

"Whatever! You wish you had Sigourney Weaver's height, short stuff."

"Just because you're an Amazon doesn't mean us regular-sized people should take shit from you. Now stop changing the subject. What gives?"

"I'm fine. Scout's honor," she said, holding up two fingers. "I guess the phone call with my editor this morning put me in a sour mood."

"Oh." Darlene winced, all teasing gone. "You got a call instead of an e-mail? This must be serious. Still no book, huh?"

"Nope. And I don't know what to do about it." She sat at the kitchen table and rested her head in her hands. The days of little sleep and lack of writing progress were finally catching up with her.

"Well, I do." Darlene removed her coat and some paperwork from her coat pocket and waved them in front of Jaime's face. "We both need a vacation, and look. Cruise information right here in my hot little hands. What do you think about a balcony?"

"I think I need coffee. Want some?"

"Jaime?"

"Huh?"

"You're doing that avoidance thing again."

"Sorry."

"No worries. And I'd love a cup." Jaime handed her a cup, refilling her own mug before sitting at the breakfast counter. "So, what do you think?"

"I *think* you're being a pain in the ass about this trip!"

"That doesn't answer my question."

"Darlene, I…can't." She didn't have the strength to fight her pain, her best friend, and the memories that surfaced every time high school came up. Overwhelmed, she felt her defenses crumble.

"Oh, honey, you can," Darlene said, kneeling in front of her. "Come on. This will be fun. Maybe you'll even rekindle some old friendships."

"You know better than anyone else I wasn't social in school. Hell, *we* didn't even become friends until after we graduated and took that stupid history course together in college. Who am I going to chat up old times with if there aren't old times to chat about?"

"Think about it this way. It's a much-needed vacation with the added benefit of maybe making some new friends. Now check out these rooms. Aren't they beautiful?"

Beautiful. A word Jaime hadn't used in a long time. She even refused to use it when she wrote. How could she, when it could only be applied to the one thing in her life that had ever meant anything to her?

Until she destroyed it.

"Jaime?"

"Oh, sorry. I did it again, didn't I?"

"Yeah, but I know this is hard for you. Come on, it'll be a blast. Besides, I know there's someone you're looking forward to seeing."

Oh, there was, a woman she'd never forget. How could she forget the way Sierra Connor used to look? Long auburn hair, deep-blue eyes, and lips the color of tree-ripened cherries. The way Sierra laughed and, damn, the way Sierra used to look at her. One glance and she'd melted like butter on a hot stove. She'd forget how to breathe before she'd forget about Sierra. But she wouldn't be caught dead on a boat. "Nope. No one."

"Bullshit! After everything you told me about Sierra Connor, you're going to sit here with that dreamy look on your face and tell me you weren't thinking about her?"

"That was the plan, yeah." She couldn't put herself through this again. The flashbacks were exactly what she was trying to avoid. She jumped to her feet, needing a way to work off some of her frustration. Pacing wasn't helping. She didn't want to talk about Sierra. Not now, not ever. "I don't want to talk about it."

"I hope you realize you suck at evasion. And what would be so wrong if you ran into her? Maybe you could talk things out."

Yeah, right. And say what? Sorry I kissed you. Sorry I lusted after you for four years and didn't say anything. Sorry I ruined our friendship by only thinking about my own feelings? "No."

"Oh, please. That was ten years ago. I'm sure she's forgiven you by now. She's probably forgotten all about it."

Jaime shut her eyes. She didn't deserve forgiveness, but the thought of Sierra forgetting her altogether made her stomach churn. She should have told Sierra how she felt, explained that she was a lesbian and she was falling for her, hard. But no. She made Sierra think their relationship was based solely on friendship. And at first, it was. "She'll never forgive me. Not that I blame her. Besides, I heard she's married and living in another state."

"That excuse is so lame. Straight women can have gay friends."

"That's not the issue. Jesus! Take a good look at my life. Even if we could be friends again, do you really think she'd want anything to do with me now? I'm an addict. I have scars that would make most people cringe. I can't even write a fucking sentence anymore. I have nothing to offer her or anyone. I'm surprised you're still my friend."

"Is drama part of being a great writer? Because you can be so theatrical sometimes." Darlene placed a hand on her shoulder to stop her from pacing. "Honey, listen to me. You're recovering from being addicted to pain medication, which by the way happens accidentally to millions of people every year. And that scar on your body doesn't put you in the Elephant Man category by any means. You're an incredible writer and unbelievably handsome. And if Sierra Connor or anyone else doesn't want to be your friend for whatever reason, then that's their loss."

"You sound like my grandmother." She swiped at a tear that rolled down her cheek.

"There's a scary thought. But if you want me to start sounding like her, I can shake my finger at you and order you to go."

She desperately wanted to believe the good things Darlene said about her and what she was capable of. Reminiscing about Sierra only made her think she had disappointed enough people in her life. Alienating the only friend she had left by not going on something like a simple cruise was ridiculous. Sierra wouldn't be there anyway—she couldn't swim well and disliked the water. What the hell. One week wouldn't kill her. "So, what were you saying about a balcony?"

"Woo-hoo!" Darlene said, jumping up and down. "You'll go?"

"Yes. Make the damn call before I change my mind."

CHAPTER TWO

Sierra Connor settled into the standard eight-by-ten cubicle, kicking back in her ergonomic chair to enjoy her morning Starbucks double-shot espresso. Booting up her computer, she winced when her headset hooked her gold hoop earring, nearly ripping it from her ear. After adjusting the earpiece into a less sadistic position, she picked up her iPad, intent on catching up on the morning news. Work officially started in ten minutes. Plenty of time to gear up for whatever the day had in store.

Although she wasn't a morning person, she'd never complain about working the early shift. The silence made it possible to think—to work into a steady routine. Routine was her life. Without it, she'd have too much time to dwell on things she couldn't change.

Change. Another concept she was familiar with. So much had happened in the last few years to make her re-evaluate her life. She'd spent too much time thinking about what could have been, and if she could bottle and sell that wasted time, she'd be a millionaire ten times over.

Questioning every detail made her a great travel agent. It's what her boss paid her for. To create the perfect trip so that someone would enjoy every moment of their vacation and escape their hectic lives without complications. Sierra was the best at making that happen. Too bad she couldn't apply those skills to the rest of her life.

The phone almost never rang before ten. Anyone who did call early usually kept to the basic last-minute questions regarding trips that had already been booked. She glanced at the piles of travel brochures in front of her, not looking forward to the rest of the day.

Fridays were always the busiest day of the week, and now that June had officially arrived, people were scrambling to book last-minute vacation destinations.

"Sierra?"

"Yeah, Boss?" She turned to find Doug peeking around the corner of his office.

"You have someone on line one wanting to book your reunion cruise."

"This early?" *Her* reunion cruise? Yeah, right. Like this trip was her idea. She wanted nothing to do with high school or the memories associated with it. Besides, she hated boats. Anyone who had watched *Titanic* knew they were just floating disasters waiting to happen. "Okay, thanks," she said, cursing softly under her breath. She hated for something to interrupt her morning flow.

Normally she loved her job. The last three years as a top-producing agent had been rewarding and offered the financial stability she hadn't had before her divorce. Unfortunately, she'd started regretting her job choice the day Doug put her in charge of the reunion account. Evidently, Warren Littleton, their former high-school class president, had found out through Facebook that she worked for the popular travel agency. He would only work with their agency if she had been put in charge of the large account. He probably thought he was doing something nice for an ex-classmate. She refused, of course. But Doug ordered her to take the account and go on the trip whether she liked it or not. He wanted her on the cruise to ensure that the finer details were taken care of, since some of the reunion guests could become clients of the travel agency. Grumbling didn't get her anywhere. *Whatever*. At least she was getting a free vacation out of the deal.

"Hello, Bay Area Vacations," she said as cordially as possible. "Of course. Please hold on a moment while I access the files. Thank you."

She double-clicked the ship icon on her desktop, opening the reunion file. Taking a deep breath, she tried to relax as her anxiety began to mount.

Ever since being assigned the reunion account, she had been haunted by her past. True, high school hadn't been necessarily terrible, and in actuality those few special memories were currently keeping her up most nights—all of them containing one special person.

Damn. She'd managed to put this chapter of her life behind her years ago. Until a few weeks ago, she hadn't thought about Jaime Rivers at all, mainly for her own sanity. Oh, well. No use worrying about that now. What was that famous cliché? Water under the bridge. Besides, she no longer blamed Jaime, only herself. "Thank you for holding. I understand you're looking to book Templeton High School's ten-year-anniversary cruise on board the *Sun Princess* leaving the first weekend in July, correct?"

"Yes," the woman answered. "I was hoping a balcony room would still be available?"

I bet you do. Figures. There was always one vacationer who wanted the best of everything and waited until the last minute to book their reservations. Anyone who knew anything about cruising would already know that the balcony rooms were the first to go on these popular excursions. Even she'd had to settle for a room with only a window, since all the balconies had been taken over two months ago. Her professional persona in place, she went through the motions anyway.

"Let me check that for you. May I get your name?"

"Darlene Whitman."

Whitman? The name didn't ring any bells. Whoever she was, this late in the game she'd be lucky to get a room at all. Not knowing the caller's name wasn't surprising. Most of the women in her class would be married by now and carry their husband's last names.

After scanning the ship's records for rooms, she was surprised to find a room with a balcony had just become available due to a last-minute cancelation. Her finger idled above the keyboard as she contemplated whether to give it to this Darlene person or swap it for her room. Who would know? *Damn it.* Being honest sucked sometimes.

"A balcony? Sure, we have one available. Will you be traveling with anyone?"

"Perfect and yes. Another classmate."

This prompted Sierra to open up another window for the second application. "Wonderful. I'll need to get both of your names, starting with yours." She was typing in all the pertinent information when her fingers suddenly stumbled across the keyboard. "I'm sorry. Can you give me the second traveler's name one more time?"

"Sure. Jaime Rivers."

Sierra gasped. "Excuse me. Could I put you on hold again for a moment? I have another call."

"Certainly."

She jumped out of her chair and paced the tight space. All those years and not a word from Jaime, and now she was going to be stuck on a boat with her for seven days after everything Jaime had put her through?

Jaime loved the water, but a cruise, really? Cruising was a social way of traveling. Jaime had never been a social person and had tried to avoid crowds at all costs. Had she changed that much over the years or was it one more thing that Sierra didn't know about her after four solid years of friendship?

Inhaling deeply, she turned her attention back to the blinking red light. No more reminiscing. The past had to remain in the past and it was time to get back to business. "I apologize for the wait. Where were we?"

Ten minutes later, she thanked the caller and said her good-byes, ignoring how sultry and genuinely nice the woman sounded. The moment the intrusive caller disconnected, she allowed the anger to surface.

Closing her eyes, she tried to swallow the burning lump in her throat. Her chest constricted. She was seconds from losing it. Who was this mystery woman making Jaime's reservations? A friend? A lover? Jaime's solitary nature made her wonder if this woman was the reason Jaime decided to go on the cruise in the first place. She knew Jaime wouldn't be caught dead on that boat unless she was being coaxed into it. Suddenly, the pain erupted into hot, flowing tears.

Jaime had spent time doing two things in high school. She liked to surf and she hung out with Sierra. She couldn't forget the countless times she'd tagged along with Jaime as she made frequent trips to a popular West-Coast beach. Visions of Jaime in her board shorts and bikini top, riding the famous Pacifica waves half an hour from San Mateo, still made her shiver. She'd stifled many screams when Jaime maneuvered too close to the rocks or when another more inexperienced surfer had cut her off and knocked her from her board. Jaime had never been a vocal person. In fact, shy and reclusive were better adjectives. But the surfing world was Jaime's universe and she'd been the Supreme Being. She'd ruled those waves and had no problem voicing her opinion regarding another surfer's stupidity.

Jaime had been a natural on her board—her toned athletic body controlling her motions as if she were part of the sea. A good four inches taller than Sierra's five foot six, Jaime seemed to stand before her now, the water dripping down her tanned body, those intense emerald-green eyes focused on her every move. Sierra never questioned why she always wanted to be with Jaime. Spending time with her was as natural as breathing. They'd been inseparable for four years and all that didn't change until the day of their graduation.

"Ten years, Jaime. Why now?" she murmured.

"You say something?" her boss asked, stopping in front of her cubicle. His look of concern meant that she'd been caught wallowing. "What's wrong?"

"Nothing."

"Sierra, I hate to state the obvious but you're crying."

"I'm fine, Boss."

Doug glared at Sierra's phone as though that would help. "Did the person on the phone upset you?"

"No, no," she said quickly, drying the tears with her shirtsleeve. "Just some old memories. I need a sec to pull myself together." Damn it. This was exactly what she was trying to avoid. All those years she'd blocked out her past, and it just took a ten-minute phone call to bring it all crashing back.

"Are you sure?"

"Positive."

"Okay. How about a refill then?" He pointed to her empty mug. "My wife says caffeine is a cure-all."

"I knew I loved Catherine for a reason." She handed him her mug and offered a reassuring smile. "Coffee would be wonderful. Thank you."

As soon as the front door closed behind him, she allowed the tears to surface again. At one time in her life all she'd known was Jaime. She'd trusted her and always felt safe when Jaime was close.

And then Jaime kissed her.

Talk about shock. A kiss had been the last thing she expected. But suddenly everything became clear. All the parties they'd skipped. All the dances they hadn't attended because Jaime would rather be alone with her and do something as simple as watch a movie. All those years of sleeping over at each other's houses and Jaime not once feeling comfortable changing in front of her. She even remembered making a joke about it. It explained why, right before prom, Jaime turned pale in the dressing room while Sierra was trying on dresses. Jaime had excused herself, saying she wasn't feeling well.

The day Jaime kissed her, Sierra had panicked. She accused Jaime of all kinds of things, unfair accusations she regretted later, all of which came from nothing more than teenage confusion. When the shock had worn off a week later, she went to Jaime's house to talk. But it was too late. A neighbor finally told her that Jaime had gone on an extended vacation with her father—a vacation Sierra knew Jaime hadn't planned to take in the first place. How could Jaime not tell her she was gay? Was their entire friendship based on a lie, and how many women had she been with?

Ruling the waves wasn't Jaime's only talent. She'd also been the master of avoidance. If it wasn't for Sierra cajoling her into spilling what was on her mind most of the time, she wouldn't have known anything about her. Weeks later, when Sierra needed to leave to attend Wisconsin State, she had never felt so alone, so lost, as she did without her best friend there to see her off. Sure, she might have hurt her by some of the things she'd said, but at least she had the guts to come back and face her.

Why hadn't she seen the signs? Jaime never wanted to socialize or hang out with other people. She didn't get along with any of Sierra's other friends. Then there were the innocent touches, a soft brush of hands or an occasional hug that sometimes left her breathless. She didn't understand what was happening at the time, but years later when she'd finally come to terms with her own sexuality, she'd realized why her body responded to Jaime the way it did. Why it was still responding to the distant memories that roared back with the simple memory of that one touch.

"You're not going to prom?" Sierra asked, surprised. "Why not?"

"There's just no one I want to go with."

"But Jaime, you have to go." She sat close to Jaime on the bed and gripped her hand. "Please, talk to me. I know something's wrong. I can feel it."

Jaime pulled her hand away and ran it through her short, spiked blond hair. "Nothing's wrong. I just...don't want to go."

Jaime couldn't hide her trembling or the fear in those piercing green eyes. Something really was wrong but Sierra couldn't get her to open up. The last few months, Jaime had been noticeably different around her, and she still had no clue as to why. "Is it something I've done?" she asked, near tears.

Jaime pulled her into a hug and rested her chin on her shoulder. "Don't cry, and no, it doesn't have anything to do with you."

"Then why are you so distant lately? Don't you want to be my friend anymore?"

"I'll always be your friend," Jaime said, hugging her tight. "You have my word."

"Well, we know how good your word is, don't we, Jaime?"

"Talking to yourself again," Doug said, pushing through the door. He handed her the steaming brew and rested with his elbow on the cubicle.

"Yep, you know me. Who needs friends when I can answer my own questions?"

He laughed. "I'll get you the card of my wife's therapist. Looks like you're going to need it."

"Thanks, Boss. How thoughtful of you."

"Anything I can do to help," he said, disappearing into his office after gently squeezing her shoulder.

Sierra slid down in her chair, cradling the mug of coffee against her, trying to chase away the chill crawling along her spine. Things could have been so different if Jaime had opened up to her about her feelings. Maybe she wouldn't have walked out on Jaime only to have Jaime disappear on her. The pity party into her past was seriously pissing her off. She'd let Jaime go a long time ago. So why did the mere mention of Jaime's name make her want to break things? The answer was simple. Jaime had a lover and she didn't. Jaime had moved on and she still didn't know how.

"I can't believe this," she mumbled, throwing her headset onto the desk. She glanced around the empty office, hoping Doug didn't hear her speak to the air again. One more time and she wouldn't be surprised to find the loony wagon waiting outside.

Touching her computer screen, she ran her fingertip slowly over Jaime's name. Imagining it was Jaime's lips instead, she traced each letter, wishing she was caressing the lips that had once kissed her senseless. How was she going to spend seven days on a cruise with Jaime and her lover, especially after coming to grips in the last few years with her own sexuality? It had taken her years to put that one kiss into perspective. At one point she'd even tried to fight it, tried to tell herself it was only Jaime who made her feel that way. She'd even married a man to prove her point.

Marriage. Talk about an ugly time in her life. She should have known after being with Eric sexually for the first time that being with a man wasn't what excited her. She'd never liked the way men felt or smelled. Everything about being with a man turned her off, and when she finally took the time to recall the last time she'd actually been turned on, it was in her bedroom, with Jaime touching her.

She'd dated a handful of women since her divorce, but none of them could ignite that special spark. Enough of a spark, sure, to let her know she preferred women to men. But after about a half-dozen dates she started believing that she was actually the problem. Why couldn't any of them make her happy? She'd been so hypercritical she'd almost given up on the idea of dating altogether.

And then she'd received her reunion letter and everything made sense. Without realizing it, she'd been comparing every woman she dated to Jaime and that first kiss. The first one wasn't tall enough and the second not tan enough. Woman number three had brown eyes and not green. The list went on and on. In her last attempt at dating she'd almost slept with the woman, but when the woman leaned forward to kiss her, she remembered her first kiss with a woman being softer, gentler. Of course that kiss had been with Jaime.

A genie could fix all her problems. One wish and she'd be back in that room all those years ago and have her second chance with Jaime. She would have recognized her own feelings—accepted her sexuality and thrown herself into Jaime's arms and never let go. Instead, ten years later she was divorced, alone, and still thinking about what could have been. At least she had a good job that paid the bills. Dabbing under her puffy eyes with a Kleenex, she was about to suggest to her boss that she needed a break when he appeared behind her.

"Okay, you need to tell me what's up. Maybe I can help," he said, placing a hand on her shoulder.

"I doubt it. God! I'm a blubbering idiot today. Must be hormonal."

"Oh…well…maybe I can't help with *that*."

"Don't worry," she said, and laughed at his rosy cheeks. She loved playing the feminine card when she needed to change the subject. Worked every time. "I won't go postal. I guess everything's catching up with me. To tell you the truth, I don't know if I can make this cruise. I have so much to do here and—"

"Stop. Right. There." Doug pointed sternly at her. "You need this. It's only a week and we'll be fine without you."

She glanced at Jaime's information on the screen. They might survive without her but she didn't think she'd survive the trip, not after finding out about Jaime and her partner. Oh, well. She'd vowed to move on, and a cruise through the Caribbean would prove she'd done just that. No more wallowing. "Okay, if you're sure. Would you mind if I take an early break? I need some fresh air."

"Of course. Take as long as you need."

"Thanks."

"Sierra," he said once more, "you sure you're okay?"

Fucked up. Insecure. Neurotic. Emotional. "Yeah, I'm fine."

❖

"Did you book it?" Jaime asked, suddenly feeling apprehensive. Maybe telling Darlene to sign them up for the cruise wasn't a smart idea. Maybe if she hung up now she could avoid Darlene for the next month and miss the cruise altogether?

"Yep, all set. By the way, I can hear the worry in your voice. Relax. We leave in thirty days. Pack your bathing suit, pal, we're going to the Caribbean!"

Bathing suit. As if. "Woo-hoo."

Darlene laughed. "You'll see. You'll be thanking me when this trip is over."

Yeah, right. Fat chance of that happening.

"I can still hear you."

"Get out of my head then."

"But there's so much room in there with all that empty space."

"Yeah, that's right, jokester," Jaime said. "Keep talking and you'll be traveling solo."

"Whatever! You're all talk. I'll call you next week. Love ya."

Jaime moved to her bookcase and reached above her head, choosing a familiar black book covered in dust. Running her hand over the smooth surface, she skimmed through the pages, stopping on the many images that always brought a smile to her face. It had been years since she dared return in time, yet she knew exactly where to find the pictures that haunted her.

Turning to the senior-class portraits, she ran her finger over the familiar figure staring back at her. She'd wanted to kiss those lips for years, but when she had, her worst fears had come to pass. Placing the book back in its resting place, she sadly realized that no matter how much time passed, feelings never changed when someone broke your heart.

Chapter Three

Jaime stared out of the passenger window of the van, taking in the never-ending stretch of highway that connected southwest Orlando with Cape Canaveral. The fifty-three-mile expanse of road passed over the intracoastal waterway, giving her sweeping views of the natural inlets and marshland. From her window, she recognized Orlando International Airport, which meant they were fast approaching the port. The weather was hot and humid, typical July weather for the Sunshine State. The air conditioning kept the temperature inside the van comfortable for the ten-or-so passengers, and she'd actually been enjoying the ride until the ship came into view.

Her idea of a vacation was a quiet tropical beach in the middle of nowhere, alone, not a ship filled with thousands of people. She'd heard the boat was big, but mammoth would have been a better description. It floated before her like those over-sized marshmallows she liked to add to her cup of hot chocolate, and she swallowed an impending anxiety attack.

The *Sun Princess* was equivalent to a floating city. More than three-thousand passengers would be on their seven-day sail, five hundred of those guests made up of reunion gatherers. Hopefully, she could avoid most of them. At least that was her intention. She'd do just enough to keep Darlene happy, but nothing more.

After checking in their luggage and showing all appropriate identification at the terminal, they received their ship's card and were escorted out to the gangplank, where they took their Welcome Aboard picture. The closer she came to boarding the vessel, the more her insides trembled. The last time she'd shaken this much, San Francisco had been experiencing an earthquake.

"Jesus, Darlene! What the hell did you get me into?"

"Wow! Isn't this incredible?"

Not quite the word she would have used. "You don't find it a little ridiculous that, after only five minutes, you have me walking the plank?"

"Actually, since you mentioned it, that is pretty funny. And if you keep complaining, I'm going to make you jump."

They followed the crowd to the Promenade Deck, where they awaited instructions to go to their rooms. It took less than fifteen minutes for Darlene to become bored with the whole waiting idea, so she decided to check out the ship while Jaime sat in a lounge chair overlooking the harbor.

"Excuse me, ma'am."

"Yes," Jaime said.

"We were just informed that all rooms are ready."

"Thanks."

"My pleasure."

Slinging her leather carry-on over her shoulder, she was about to go search for Darlene when she ran into one of her former classmates, who hadn't changed at all in the past ten years. In fact, the last time Jaime had seen that much plastic surgery performed on a woman she was at a Cher concert.

"Jaime!"

She tensed as the woman pulled her into an awkward hug. "Uh…hi."

The woman's laugh was as annoying as it'd been in high school. The cackle made the hairs stand up on the back of her neck, the sound still as ear-piercing. "You don't remember me, do you?"

"Actually, Marcy, I remember you quite well."

Marcy DuPont had been head cheerleader for Templeton High School and the class's chief gossip queen. She made it her business to know everything about everyone, which was one of the main reasons Jaime had stayed far away from her. Not to mention that she'd been the butt of many of Marcy's jokes.

"There you are," Darlene said, looping her arm through Jaime's. "Is our room ready yet, honey? Oh, hello, Marcy."

Honey?

"Darlene," Marcy said, her eyebrows raised. "How nice to see you. You two are sharing a room?"

Jaime fidgeted under Marcy's scrutiny. The woman had always made her nervous. The familiar twinkle in her eyes suggested that by dinner, the whole ship would know they were sharing a room and most likely *other* activities, if Marcy put her usual spin on the details. It obviously wasn't a secret that Jaime was gay, but she didn't want Darlene to become part of the many rumors that Marcy would most likely start on the ship.

"Yes, we are. Aren't we, sweetie?" Darlene said, kissing her sweetly on the cheek.

She registered the gentle squeeze on her arm, Darlene's way of alerting her to play along. Cool. If Darlene wanted to play the happy couple for the whole trip, the week might not be so boring after all. Just seeing the priceless expression on Marcy's face the moment Darlene called her sweetie was worth the cost of the cruise alone. "That's right, *baby*. They said our room's all set."

"Perfect. And I can't wait to get there. See ya around, Marcy."

She had a hard time keeping a straight face as Darlene dragged her toward the elevators. As soon as the elevator doors closed, they broke into a fit of laughter.

"I told you you'd thank me when this cruise is over," Darlene said, holding her sides. "Did you see that mannequin's face? I was afraid it would crack when she smiled!"

"Ouch," she said, laughing harder. "That's rough even for you."

"Get real. I bet she could blink her lips if she tried. Besides, I saw that evil glare. I bet you by dinnertime, she'll tell everyone she saw us having sex or something on our balcony."

"And you're okay with that?"

"Fuck her. The last thing I'm going to worry about is Marcy DuPont. Come on. Let's go check out our room."

They arrived at the tenth floor, finding their luggage waiting for them by the door. She immediately scoped out their balcony, planning to spend a lot of time enjoying the sun on the privacy of their own deck.

"Well, what do you think?"

"You were right about the deck. This is perfect." She threw her suitcases onto one of the beds and sprawled out next to them.

"I knew you'd like it. Let's go check out the pool and sauna area. I only made it as far as the buffet before they announced the rooms were ready."

She pulled a magazine out of her suitcase and kicked off her shoes. She figured she'd do a little reading and then take a nap before dinner. "Nah, that's okay. You go without me." When Darlene didn't move, she looked up to find her staring pointedly at her. "What?"

"What do you mean what? Do you have any idea where you are?"

"Uh…yeah. I'm trapped on a large boat with thousands of people. I'm living a nightmare." She returned to the article regarding the women's surfing semifinals in Rio de Janeiro.

"Get up."

"Excuse me?"

"You are not allowed to hide in here. Get up."

She returned Darlene's hard stare. "Make me."

"Don't tempt me, Rivers," Darlene said, leaning over her. "Get up or I'll dump you on your ass."

"Ha! You and whose army?"

Before she knew what was happening, she found herself on the floor with Darlene looming over her and holding her bedsheet.

"Now, stop screwing around and let's go check out the boat," Darlene said, throwing the bedsheet over Jaime's head before she exited the room.

"It's a ship," she yelled after her, counting down the seconds until their first day would come to an end.

❖

Sierra smoothed the wrinkles out of her dress, taking one more look at herself in the full-length mirror. Tonight was the first ship's dinner, the first time in ten years she would see Jaime. Maybe, if she could just get through dinner and survive seeing her with her lover, she'd be able to get through the rest of the trip. At least that was her plan.

She knew what room they shared and what table they'd been assigned to because she'd planned the whole trip right down to the excursions. If she'd calculated things properly, she'd be able to avoid running into Jaime everywhere except dinner.

Since the phone call with Jaime's lover, she had done nothing but wonder where Jaime was and what she was doing. Of course, her fantasies didn't include Jaime having a lover. She even managed to convince herself that maybe Jaime really wasn't involved in a relationship. Maybe the woman was a friend. But what was the likelihood of that? Jaime had been incredibly attractive in high school, and if she still surfed or worked out in any way, her body would have to be perfect. She couldn't imagine Jaime looking like some of the other women from her class that she'd already run into on the cruise. Most of them were married or divorced with kids. They either worked out so much they were too skinny or pregnancy hadn't treated their bodies with respect. She couldn't picture Jaime with kids, but hell, that didn't mean she didn't have any. Until a month ago, she couldn't picture Jaime agreeing to go on this cruise either. Apparently, Jaime was still an enigma.

She applied the last of her makeup then headed to the dining room, only to be stopped by dozens of former classmates, most of them clearly shocked as to how stunning she'd turned out. In school, she'd been thin, lanky, and awkward. She'd even worn glasses in a feeble attempt to hide, not because she'd really needed them. She never stood out from the crowd—didn't hang out with the popular people, which was probably one of the many reasons she had been attracted to Jaime from the start. But in that moment, in that dress, showing off her hard-won curves, she knew she was hard to miss. And she felt good. Really good.

The form-fitting black cocktail dress flowed around her curves, and with each sway of her hips she exuded a confidence she didn't actually feel, although she knew she looked great. She'd replaced her glasses with contacts about five years ago and recently styled her auburn hair to fall in soft waves around her face. She wore it longer than she had in high school, the dark locks a nice contrast to her blue eyes, or so she hoped. If she wanted to lie to herself, she could say that she did it because she wanted to impress her classmates or that she wanted to feel good about herself. But deep down she knew that she was dressed to kill only because she wanted Jaime to see what she'd missed if they happened to run into one another.

A large crowd had gathered outside the main dining hall as the two large mahogany doors opened to admit the guests. She immediately found her seat next to the large ornate spiral staircase that led to the first-story dining section. There she could see that Jaime's table was still unoccupied, but that didn't stop the butterflies from flapping excitedly in her stomach. She'd decided to seat herself with seven other single classmates, regretting her choice immediately as they started gathering around the circular table.

Tracy Paterson and Joyce Wilhemson hadn't changed since high school, the latest class gossip already spilling from their mouths. It didn't escape her notice that Jaime's name had been instantly mentioned, and when Tracy hinted about the kiss that Jaime had received in front of Marcy DuPont earlier that day, Sierra suddenly lost her appetite.

Six hours on the ship and already the class gossips were spinning their tales. Regardless of their past and who Jaime was with, she felt the sudden need to protect her. Even though they were only rumors, sadness plagued her because all rumors had a little truth to them. She didn't want to think about Jaime kissing anyone, so she turned to her other tablemates in an attempt to change the topic.

Barkley O'Brien, Megan Stevenson, and Larry Crocker were all divorced and appeared to be on the prowl for their next spouse. They'd been scouring the room incessantly since they sat down, and it seemed that Megan had already taken a seat next to some poor unsuspecting sap at a nearby table. The final two classmates, whose names were failing her at the moment, hadn't appeared yet, and just as she was about to excuse herself to use the restroom, she spotted the only person in the world who had the power to upend her world.

Chapter Four

Jaime followed the maître d' to their assigned table, trailed closely by Darlene. The distinct ringing of glasses being bumped against each other in salutation signaled that the formal dining room was open for dinner. She took time to admire the tasteful décor while carefully avoiding bumping into one of the dozen waiters rushing about. Large crystal chandeliers hung from the tall ceilings, emitting a subtle glow. Classical music poured from the corner speakers, and waiters smiled and took orders from the many guests that would be in their care for the next week. Two-person tables outlined the bottom half of the two-story room, and Jaime prayed they'd be seated at one. Nope. Instead, it took all her willpower not to say, "Are you fucking kidding me?" when the maitre d' stopped in front of a circular table smack in the center of the packed room.

Jesus! What higher power did I piss off to deserve this? If going on this cruise wasn't bad enough, here she was sharing a table with three ex-football players and their wives. One of the couples was the gossiping Marcy DuPont and her equally obnoxious husband, Bo Tyson.

As the group of men slapped each other on the backs and the women placed fake kisses into the air, she was nauseated at their phony displays of affection. Thankfully it had happened before dinner; otherwise keeping her meal down would have been next to impossible. To top it off, one of the women turned and pulled her into a tight embrace, like they'd been friends forever. She stiffened, and as she threw Darlene a "you're going to pay for this later" look, she decided the cruise had just gone from being a category-one storm to a disaster of biblical proportions.

"Jaime Rivers, I didn't think I'd see you on this ship," Bo Tyson said, placing an arm around his wife.

She stifled a laugh at the possessive gesture. As if she'd ever make a play for Ms. Plastic Tits. "That makes two of us, Bo."

People like Bo Tyson were one of the many reasons she'd mentally blocked out high school. As he sat before her with a shit-eating grin on his face, memories of all those days he'd made her life hell roared back. A week confined with all these people on a ship and now she had to deal with this clown? It had to be the boat gods' idea of a sick joke.

"Do your cheeks ache?" Darlene said under her breath.

"Why do you ask?"

"That unusual toothy expression. Kind of freaky, if you ask me. I can tell you want to kill him, but try to be good."

"This is me being good," she murmured, deciding to say as little as possible through the rest of the meal.

Boring idle chatter consumed the table as Jaime pushed her food aimlessly around on her plate. As she suspected, the topic was high school—rehashing the glory days like they'd occurred yesterday. No matter how hard she tried, she couldn't block out the memories that the stories produced. How could she forget that she'd built her life around Sierra, only to have it come crumbling down around her? But hey, on the flip side, she'd spent four enjoyable years with the only person that had ever connected with her on so many levels. Maybe waiting until the last day of school to spill her guts had been a good choice after all; otherwise they might never have shared so many great years. Looking back, she still couldn't figure out how she'd mustered up the courage to kiss Sierra. Impulsiveness had never been her strong suit. Honestly, avoiding anything of a personal nature was more her style. But something had drawn her to Sierra that day, something she hadn't experienced since. She sighed and stabbed at her salad.

Three glasses of wine later, Marcy and her friends excused themselves to use the ladies' room. The second they were out of earshot, an inebriated Bo Tyson turned his attention to Jaime.

"So, Rivers. When did you two," he pointed his glass at Darlene, "hookup?"

His arrogant tone made her clench her fist under the table. She'd promised Darlene she'd be civil and she wouldn't break her promise. That didn't mean she wouldn't kill Darlene later for subjecting her to this dinner torture. "A while ago."

"Ooh, look at you getting all defensive." Bo laughed. "I'm just saying. She doesn't seem your type, but neither did that scrawny little thing back in school. Oh, what was her name? Sierra…yeah, that's it."

She couldn't figure out what was more painful, her jaw from gritting her teeth or that Bo dared bring up Sierra's name in any context. There'd been a lot of speculation in school about her and Sierra's relationship, but she had avoided the hearsay because she'd never wanted Sierra to find out that there was some truth to all the conjecture. Risking her friendship back then wasn't an option, but since then, quite a bit had changed. One being her willingness to speak up against the Bo Tyson's of the world. "Look, Bo—"

"Jaime, no." Darlene placed her hand on her thigh to quiet her. "What's wrong, Tyson?" she asked, leaning into Jaime. "Jealous she could give me what you could never offer a woman?"

"Jealous?" He sneered. "Of a lesbo? You've got to be joking? Besides, if you tasted this," he said pointing to his body, "you'd never go back to that."

"That's a tempting offer," Darlene said. "But sorry. Not into the shriveled-up beef-jerky types."

Jaime's unrestrained laughter was infectious, as the rest of the table laughed along with her. She threw her arm around Darlene. *That's my girl. Let him have it.*

"You got humor, Darlene. I dig it," Bo said, but the slight twitch to his jaw suggested he didn't find her comment funny at all. "Obviously, though, you wouldn't kid if you'd tried out my manly attributes." He flexed one of his biceps, making his friends laugh.

"Okay, I think that's enough," Jaime said, not enjoying the teasing any longer. "Let's enjoy the rest of our dinner."

"It's fine, honey." Darlene squeezed her hand for reassurance under the table. "Don't listen to him. He's had a little too much tonight. Besides, his 'manly attributes,' as he calls them, can't compare to what you give me."

She should have known Darlene could take care of herself. The crimson color of Bo's face suggested he was pissed, but she couldn't tell if it was because of Darlene's quick comeback or their well-played-out happy-couple routine.

"You'd be surprised what I could give you—"

"Bo," Joey Richards said. "You're drawing a crowd. Come on, bring it down a notch, dude."

Bo quickly scanned the nearby tables and smiled at the couple behind him, who, judging by the look of disapproval on their faces, had evidently overheard the entire conversation. He placed his napkin back into his lap and adjusted his tie. "You're right. My apologies, ladies. I was out of line."

She wasn't buying his bullshit apology or his sham attempt at manners, but she was willing to give Joey a few kudos for making Bo back off. The perfect-gentleman routine couldn't work for someone like Bo, who was anything but. Getting on Bo's bad side usually meant trouble, but as the ripples of tension faded, she figured it was her cue to leave before they swelled once again. "Honey, I think it's time for some fresh air." She stood, extending her hand to Darlene. "Join me?"

"No, I'll be fine. Oh goody, look. Dessert and coffee have arrived. Go. Have fun."

"Are you sure?"

Her willingness to play the relationship game for all it was worth had been fun, but she'd had enough excitement for one night. Besides, she was entertaining thoughts of wringing Bo's neck, although, taking into account the way it hung over the collar of his shirt, she'd need hands the size of Bigfoot.

"I'm sure. Catch ya later." Darlene pulled her into a quick embrace. "Go relax," she whispered before kissing her cheek.

The only way Darlene would ever catch her later was if she returned to their room. She needed air, but what she really needed was off the damn boat. Could this vacation get any worse?

Sierra remained transfixed by the tall athletic figure wearing white tuxedo pants and a maroon silk shirt. Jaime was still as lean as she remembered and just as handsome. Her wheat-kissed hair contrasted to her deeply tanned skin, and even from a distance Sierra could see the reflection of light dancing in Jaime's dazzling emerald eyes. Jaime's hand was extended to a smaller brunette seated next to her, but Sierra couldn't see her face because her back was to her. Obviously the woman was Jaime's partner. The thought depressed her.

Even with the physical distance between them, she recognized the familiar subtle signs of Jaime's tension. Jaime's stiff posture and tight jaw suggested she was holding on by a thread. She hadn't known Jaime to be a vocal person unless she was being protective of someone, but whatever Bo had said to her had apparently gotten under Jaime's skin. People at other tables around them kept looking at Bo, which meant he was being his usual obnoxious self. She had to look away when the brunette wrapped one arm around Jaime's shoulders and pulled her close. Of course, with Bo leering at them like a lion guarding its kill, she would have done the same thing out of a need to protect Jaime.

The room receded from view as she flashed back to a time in school when Jaime had protected her from the likes of Bo Tyson and his goons. She'd never forget that day or how safe Jaime had made her feel.

"Well, look who we have here," Bo said, backing her up against one of the school's lockers. His mouth was so close to her face, she could still smell the salami he ate for lunch. "Where's your friend?"

"I have no idea who you're talking about," she said, trying without success to push past him.

"Sure you do. You and that dyke, Rivers, are always together."

"Don't call her that!"

"You have a better word?"

"Tyson," Jaime said, reaching for her arm to pull her so she was standing behind Jaime. *"Why don't you get lost?"*

"Why don't you make me, Rivers?" he said, pointing at her chest.

It appeared Jaime was about to respond when Mr. Chilton, one of Templeton High's math teachers, appeared, quickly breaking up the crowd and eventually leaving Jaime and her alone in the hallway.

"Thanks," she said, wanting to hug Jaime. But after Bo had accused Jaime of being a lesbian she didn't want to add any more gasoline to the fire.

"You don't have to thank me. I won't ever let him or anyone hurt you."

Jaime had kept that promise all through school. She had purposely seated Jaime and her lover at Tyson's table because she was childishly jealous of their relationship, and suddenly she felt foolish and petty. Sure, she was still angry with Jaime, but she couldn't bear to see her get hurt by tangling with three-hundred-pound Bo Tyson. Even from across the room, the tension at their table was palpable. Bo had been the reason that Templeton High made it to the State Conference Championship. His broad shoulders and bulging neckline made him look like The Thing from the Fantastic Four, and considering Jaime's lean body, he could snap her in half with a single flick of his wrist.

Unable to watch their table any longer, she excused herself and headed outside. The closing of the automatic doors offered a tangible barrier between the dining room and the outside world. Swiping angrily at her tears, she knew she'd been mistaken to think that seeing Jaime happy with someone else would somehow free her from the past. She'd wanted to think she'd made the right decision to not have contacted Jaime over the years. That had been her intention anyway. But seeing Jaime happy and looking as good, if not better, than she had ten years ago, made her realize she'd only been fooling herself.

The rhythmic crashing of the waves against the side of the ship helped clear her head—anything to erase the images of Jaime in the arms of another woman. How was she going to survive night after night watching Jaime and her lover hang all over each other? Every time that woman touched Jaime, she suffered the loss of their friendship again. As if the memories weren't painful enough, reality just plain sucked.

She pulled her shawl tighter around her shoulders as she tried to fight the chill that had nothing to do with being cold. Feeling as though someone was watching her, she turned and froze.

❖

"Sierra?" Jaime blinked as if to restart her brain. *No way.* How could this gorgeous creature before her, looking incredibly sexy in a black cocktail dress that fit her like a second skin, be Sierra? Her wavy auburn hair was a bit longer but the color exactly as she remembered. And those eyes, those intense, perfect sapphires simply dazzling against the night sky.

Still uncertain, she slowly filled her lungs with the salty air. The ocean always calmed her, and even though she hadn't been near the sea in a while, the familiar sounds and smells still intoxicated and soothed her. She'd been staring out into the vast emptiness questioning her existence when she caught the hint of a familiar scent. Spice with a hint of spring flowers. Kenzo. Sierra.

"I can't believe this," she said. "Is it really you?"

"Yeah, it is."

Without thinking about the consequences of the last time she'd touched Sierra, she opened her arms wide as Sierra flung herself into them and let out a small cry. Holding on tight, she hugged Sierra with the passion of years lost, afraid to let go—afraid that if she did, Sierra would somehow disappear again.

A tidal wave of emotions slammed into her, knocking the breath from her chest. Joy. Sadness. Longing. Fear. Each emotion pounded into her until she began to drown from the overpowering sensations. When the realization hit that they would all eventually lead to heartbreak, she finally broke free and gasped for air, severing their fragile connection.

"What's wrong?" Sierra asked, placing her palm on her face. "You're pale."

"No…nothing. Shocked, I guess." *Oh, God don't touch me right now. I can barely stand as it is.*

"Why? Didn't expect me to be here?"

Sierra removed her hand as she swayed, suffering the loss instantly. "Honestly…no."

"It *is* our reunion."

She tried not to stare. Sierra's black strapless dress was a perfect fit. Dipping at the neckline, it offered an enticing look at her generous cleavage. Sierra was nothing like the skinny teenager she remembered. Sure, she'd been attractive back then. But now, she was drop-dead gorgeous.

Realizing she'd been staring at Sierra's breasts, she let her eyes travel upward until they focused on Sierra's. Those eyes were exactly as she remembered—razor sharp and laser blue. When Sierra narrowed those eyes, instinct warned her to take a step back.

"Well, aren't you going to answer my question?"

"No…I…." She wasn't prepared for the onslaught of emotions. Sierra wasn't supposed to be here. What should she say or, for that matter, do? Should she apologize? Say it was all a mistake. *Think, damn it!*

"How about I go first?" Sierra said, placing her hands on her hips. "Let me start with, I am so mad at you."

She looked away. "I know. I'm sorry." This was exactly the reaction she'd expected, though it didn't make it easier to deal with. Maybe an apology was in order.

"Sorry? You're *sorry*? You leave without so much as a good-bye and that's all you have to say to me after all this time?"

Wait. *What?* Sure, Sierra had every right to be mad at her for the kiss and for lying to her, but to be angry because she left? "Come again. You're mad at *me* for leaving? Who walked out on who?"

"I may have walked out, but at least I came back!"

"What are you talking about? No, you didn't. I waited a week to hear from you. Jesus, Sierra. You said you couldn't trust me, that you never wanted to see me again. You couldn't even look at me," she said, her voice breaking.

"I did come back." Sierra took a hesitant step forward but didn't touch her. "Look, I know what I said. I never meant—"

"Excuse me," someone said as they approached, unmindful of the conversation they'd interrupted. "Aren't you Jaime Rivers, the author?"

She stared at the two young giggling women. Talk about bad timing. "Yes," she said, trying to hide her frustration.

"I knew it," the other one said excitedly. "You write the Flynn Russell series. I love those stories."

"I'm glad you like them."

She turned to find Sierra standing back a few feet, watching the exchange with interest. She didn't want to be rude to a few of her fans, but she really wanted to hear what Sierra had to say. She was about to politely ask the two women if she could get their names and leave them a signed copy of her book at the reception desk, but three of their fellow reunion people had walked out onto the deck and engaged Sierra in conversation. They were all hugging each other in greeting, but Sierra's eyes remained locked on her. She rubbed her arms as if cold, the distance in Sierra's gaze dissipating the heat once felt between them. She wanted to approach her again, but not with all those other people around.

"Could I get your autograph?" the taller one asked, holding out a napkin and a pen.

As Sierra turned and wandered away with a few of their classmates, leaving no more chance for further discussion, the recognizable void left by Sierra's absence returned full force, returning her to familiar, if unwelcome, ground.

"Yeah, sure."

CHAPTER FIVE

Jaime tossed and turned, the gentle rocking of the ship doing nothing to soothe her. Like flashes on a movie screen, images of Sierra flickered behind her eyelids all night long. Tired and restless, she quietly threw on some clothes so she wouldn't wake Darlene and went in search of an early breakfast.

The ship was deserted at six a.m. so finding a secluded spot outside on the buffet deck was no problem. Her growling stomach reminded her that she hadn't finished her dinner the night before. At one point she'd thought about ordering a late-night snack, but the butterflies had been fluttering wildly since she'd run into Sierra, and eating when she was nervous was normally impossible. Since her anxiety hadn't quieted she was surprised when the glass of milk didn't sour the second it hit her stomach.

Rolling her head from side to side, she tried to work out the kinks in her neck that always surfaced when she was stressed. After a few distinct pops, she rested against her lounge chair and closed her eyes, breathing in the soothing smells of salt and early morning sunshine blowing in from the Atlantic. But as soon as she slipped into a semi-relaxed state, images of Sierra resurfaced. The emotional turmoil she'd suffered since running into Sierra made her wonder if she'd get a good night's sleep for the rest of the trip. How could she relax when she'd most likely be bumping into her at dinners, shows, or simply strolling on deck? She couldn't stand there like she had last night, with her mouth hanging open, unable to answer a simple question. Sierra must have thought she'd lost her mind. Given the way Sierra had looked in that dress, Jaime was lucky she hadn't started drooling. But somewhere on the ship, Sierra was sound asleep with her *husband*. Talk about having a whole new perspective on things. Not only was Sierra straight, she was married. Straight and married. Finding a way to keep her distance was starting to sound more appealing by the second.

What really got under her skin, besides the fact Sierra was married, was that Sierra had the gall to be mad at her when it was Sierra who had walked away all those years ago. She'd waited a week to hear from Sierra, but the hours and days had crawled by with no word. Jaime wasn't stupid. She'd accepted that she'd stepped over a line she should have never crossed. She had seen the tortured look in Sierra's eyes, the vacant expression that had haunted her for months after she left town. If Sierra only knew how it had killed her to go on vacation with her father that summer, what it had felt like as the miles stretched between them, knowing that Sierra wanted nothing more to do with her ever again.

At the time, she had contemplated discussing the issue of Sierra with her dad but just as quickly squashed that idea. Her dad was career military. In her house that meant "don't ask, don't tell" was the respected policy. She could have never discussed sex with him, or worse, her sexuality, given his strict military ideals. Looking back, it was probably one reason she avoided anything personal and never wanted to share her emotional state with anyone. Undoubtedly she'd inherited those traits from her father. He'd always told her that emotions were better kept in check and that they were for the weak. Emotions flawed your judgment. Revealing your flaws made you vulnerable. She'd learned the last one the hard way by kissing Sierra and finally telling her how she felt about her. Dad had been right. That little lapse in judgment had cost Jaime her best friend.

She'd wished many times during those awkward teenage years that her mother had stuck around. Sure, she'd missed her all the time since her mom bailed on them when she was five, but maybe if she'd been there when she needed her most they could have talked. A woman's perspective could have shed new light on her situation—helped her get through one of her most devastating teenage moments. That absence had always rung hollow in Jaime's life. Even now, she still wished she'd known why her mom had left without so much as a good-bye.

"Jaime?"

There it was again—that velvety smooth voice with the power to melt icebergs, which still had the same effect on her even after all these years. That same voice had thrown her into a tailspin merely twelve hours ago. With her eyes still closed she took a few calming breaths and hoped that when she opened them she wouldn't witness the same look of anger and resentment on Sierra's face from the night before.

Sierra's familiar floral scent carried on the ocean breeze, prompting her to open her eyes. Slowly she acknowledged Sierra with a slow scan up the shapely legs that disappeared under a short blue sarong. By the time her eyes locked on Sierra's, Sierra was shaking her head.

"Think I was a twenty-year-old groupie?" Sierra placed her hands on her hips.

"Actually, no." She dropped her eyes back to Sierra's legs. "With those legs, I would have guessed nineteen tops."

"Very smooth, Rivers. I guess all the ladies fall for that line?"

"No." She grinned. "Not all of them."

"Anyone sitting here?"

"At the moment, no."

Sierra sat and placed her coffee cup on the table before picking it up again and fiddling with it. An uncomfortable silence settled between them like a wet blanket. "Well, aren't you going to say something?" Sierra finally asked.

"Sure." She shrugged noncommittally. "How have you been?"

Sierra bit her lip, then rose. "I'm sorry," she said, tears clouding her eyes. "I can't do this with you. Good-bye, Jaime."

"No!" She grabbed Sierra's arm. "Please, don't go. I'm sorry."

"Why not, if we're going to sit here and act like we've just met?"

"Because I don't want you to go. I really want to get to know you again, honest. You just seem so…hell, I don't know…distant, I guess would be a good word."

"I'm distant?" Sierra said, her tone incredulous. "Coming from the person who's always avoided anything personal, that's rich. And even if that were true, what the hell did you expect?" She wiped at the stubborn tears with the back of her hand. "You won't talk to me, and when you do it's cryptic. Do you really care so little about me that we can't be friends anymore?"

Friends? Talk about their conversation taking another surprising turn. "I never wanted to *stop* being your friend. I made a mistake, and it cost us our friendship. I know that and I'm sorry. But it wasn't *me* that walked away. That keeps trying to walk away."

"I see," Sierra said, suddenly finding a spot on the deck interesting.

"Look." She rubbed the bridge of her nose, trying to get her thoughts in order. "Can we start over? I would really like it if we could get along since we're stuck on this damn ship for the next week. What do you say?"

Jaime touched her on the shoulder as Sierra looked up and narrowed her eyes. "That look isn't going to work on me, Rivers."

"I have no clue what you're talking about."

"Bullshit. Those puppy-dog eyes and pouty lips. You always tried to use them on me when we were teenagers. It didn't work then, so it won't work now."

"I'm surprised you remember."

"Of course I remember," Sierra said, linking her fingers through Jaime's. "Jesus, we were friends for four years—best friends. How could you think I'd forget about that? About you?"

"I'm sorry."

"Yeah, I know. You said that already. Come on. The sun's almost up. Let's go watch one of nature's most beautiful natural phenomena."

She followed Sierra to one of the ship's decks and leaned on the railing, focusing on the ocean. She wanted to touch Sierra, but the barrier between them now was as thick and cold as an Alaskan glacier. When Sierra shivered, she couldn't help but grab Sierra's hand and run her thumb over the back of it, as if that small action could ease her apparent suffering. "Cold?"

"No. But what you said earlier, I don't want you to be sorry. It was partly my fault. Maybe if—"

"There you are," Darlene said as she approached from the elevators, making both of them jump. "I've been looking everywhere for you. You left without waking me up. What gives?"

Sierra dropped her hand, withdrawing in more ways than one. Christ, what were the odds of two awkward moments with Sierra in less than twelve hours, Jaime thought as she glanced in Sierra's direction. Damn the boat gods and their sick sense of humor.

CHAPTER SIX

Sierra took a guilty step back as Jaime's partner approached. Except for the three of them standing on the deck, the boat was still relatively quiet for the early hour. When the woman stopped next to Jaime, Sierra suddenly recognized Jaime's girlfriend.

Darlene Bransen had turned into a striking brunette. The former head of their high-school debate team, Darlene was short but quick-witted and feisty. Jaime couldn't argue her way out of a parking ticket, let alone be partnered up with the best debate captain their school ever had. How the hell could these two be together? It didn't make any sense. She didn't remember registering Darlene for the cruise. She took in Darlene's proud stance and confident smile.

This woman must walk all over Jaime.

"Darlene," Jaime said, turning to make introductions. "You remember Sierra."

"Oh, hey, Sierra. Been a long time." Darlene looked curiously back and forth between them both. "I'm sorry, did I interrupt something?"

"No, that's okay," she said quickly. "We were just catching up. I should leave you two alone."

"You don't have to," Darlene said sweetly.

Jaime fidgeted like she wanted to shed her skin and crawl into a hole.

Sierra decided she would rather jump over the railing and take her chances swimming back home than watch them hang all over each other again. Last night from a distance had been one thing because she could hide her feelings. But at such a close range, she wouldn't be able to hide her hurt and disappointment, especially not from someone like Jaime, who, at one time, had known her better than anyone.

"Besides, I haven't had my coffee yet and Jaime knows how grumpy I am in the morning before caffeine. Join us so she doesn't have to deal with me by herself," Darlene said.

"Yeah, Sierra, join us," Jaime said, her tone almost pleading. "It'll give us more time to catch up."

What a sucker she was. There were those damn puppy-dog eyes again. Against her better judgment she reluctantly agreed, following Jaime and Darlene to the Seattle's Best Coffee stand located in the middle of the ship near the casino. They sat near the windows overlooking the open ocean.

"Let me get my coffee and I'll be right back," Darlene said.

She watched Darlene chatting at the coffee bar and would have never believed that she and Jaime were together unless she'd seen it with her own eyes. Weirdly, however, they acted very differently this morning than the way they had last night. Not only did Jaime not touch Darlene in any way or give her a kiss when she first showed up that morning, they actually kept a respectable distance from each other. She should have looked Jaime up on Facebook before going on the cruise so she could avoid these types of surprises, but deep down, she'd always tried to avoid looking up anything about Jaime's personal life.

If she had, she would have been prepared for things like the young women who had gathered around Jaime last night like they were starstruck. She had no idea that Jaime was a famous lesbian author or that she'd sold thousands of books and had a large fan base. After watching the way women gravitated toward Jaime and the way her partner hung all over her, she decided Jaime had everything she could possibly hope for—everything that Sierra always wanted and still didn't have. The realization cut deep.

"Sierra," Jaime said, placing a hand on her arm. "What's bothering you? You've been quiet since Darlene showed up."

"Since you mentioned it, I'm thinking that I feel like a third wheel here and that your partner is going to get upset if you keep touching me."

"Whoa!" Jaime said, clearly shocked. "Wait a sec. What gave you the idea that Darlene is my partner?"

"Well, isn't she?"

"No."

What? "Okay, I'm confused."

"You and me both." Jaime leaned closer. "Darlene isn't my partner. I don't have a partner. What makes you think I did?"

"But I saw…and people on the ship…" Heat raced across her cheeks.

"You didn't answer my question." Jaime closed the gap between them and was so close, a few strands of Sierra's hair fluttered against her face when Jaime spoke.

"I assumed. I mean…the way she touches you all the time. And then Marcy said…well I just thought you were…together."

"Marcy?" Jaime's look of surprise faded to a slow smile. "Since when did *you* ever listen to what Marcy DuPont had to say?"

Not being able to handle the warmth in Jaime's eyes and the matching tone in her voice, she looked away before the heat melted her from the inside out. Only Jaime had ever had the power to do that to her. "I don't know. I guess I should say I'm sorry. But I still can't seem to put two and two together."

"The answer is four," Jaime said, receiving a playful slap on the arm.

"God, you're such a smart-ass."

"Yep. That's one thing that'll never change," Jaime said with a quiet laugh. "And I don't want you to be sorry. Darlene and I are friends. Period. We ran into Marcy the first day on the ship and the gossip queen started asking too many questions. Since we're sharing a room, we figured we'd have a little fun with her and play into the rumor mill. Marcy, of course, didn't disappoint. Besides, I enjoyed it even more when I realized it pissed off her brain-dead husband."

She chuckled softly, feeling a little foolish and more than a little relieved. "I bet it did. How long have you two been friends? You're obviously close."

"We got to know each other after high school," Jaime said, smiling fondly at Darlene as she laughed with a former classmate who had joined her at the coffee stand.

"I'm glad you have each other."

"Me too."

"Anyone else that you've kept in touch with?"

"Not from high school. I have friends, of course, but you know me. I never did socialize much."

"I remember." Sadly, though, Jaime was wrong. Jaime was a stranger to her after all this time. "But you're a successful writer. Surely you have hundreds of people in your life? Don't you do book signings and things like that? I bet tons of people would want to get to know you."

"It's not the same." Jaime glanced away, clearly embarrassed. "Those people equate me with my character, Flynn."

She had no idea about Jaime's character because she'd never read the books. She'd downloaded the first one onto her Kindle last night the minute she returned to her room but fell asleep from exhaustion before she managed to get through the first chapter. Even so, Jaime was beautiful, brilliant, and she refused to believe that people weren't knocking down her door. "I'm sure not all of them do."

"Well, maybe not *all*, but most. My character, Flynn, is bold, daring, and handsome. She can do anything. Women flock to her. She's a hero." Jaime's voice faltered. "I'm nothing like her."

She placed her hand on Jaime's cheek, turning her face to get Jaime to look at her. "Oh, Jaime. Don't you see? I've never read any of your books but from the sound of it, Flynn is *you*."

"Yeah...well..." Jaime nervously cleared her throat.

"Hey, I'm sorry if I'm embarrassing you but it's the truth." She looked deep into Jaime's eyes, trying to convey with her steady gaze that she truly believed everything she was saying. They broke eye contact when Darlene approached with treats in hand.

"What did I miss?" Darlene asked, handing them both a cup of coffee and a croissant.

"Nothing much," Jaime said, accepting her breakfast. "Thanks."

"No problem. If that's the case would you two mind if I bug out on you? My old chemistry lab partner, Hayley Philips, wants me to go sit with her and a few of the people we used to share lab with."

"Sure," Jaime said, looking at Sierra. "We won't mind, will we?"

"Not at all. Thanks for the coffee and the pastry, by the way."

"You're welcome. And it really was great seeing you again, Sierra. Maybe you can talk this old sour puss into doing something fun with us this week," Darlene said with a playful wink as she headed to another table.

"Wow." Sierra laughed. "She's still so full of energy. How does she do it?"

"No idea. I love her like a sister, but all that energy can drive me crazy sometimes."

"Tell me more about her."

"Like what?"

"For starters, is she involved with someone else?"

"Married, actually," Jaime said, taking a sip of espresso. "Her husband, Walter, is a great guy."

"She's not gay?"

"No." Jaime shook her head, grinning. "Straight as an arrow. They've been married for three years, and Walter is one of those Silicon Valley computer nerds."

"Damn. I would have never pegged Darlene to marry a techno geek. But I guess I should have known she was married."

"How could you?"

She shifted restlessly in her chair. She'd been making the wrong assumptions about Jaime and her life since that phone call all those weeks ago. Even though she felt foolish, she owed Jaime the truth. "I was the one Darlene called that day to book the room you're sharing. I work for Bay Area Vacations. She told me her last name was Whitford. When I saw her with you, the last-name change should have clued me in that she was married."

The puzzled look on Jaime's face meant she was mentally putting the pieces of Sierra's story together. "Hold up. *You* put this all together?"

"You act surprised." She crossed her arms over her chest. "Didn't think I was smart enough to book a cruise?"

"Well…no…I mean…"

"That's right, Rivers. I want to see you squirm your way out of this one."

"Not even going to try," Jaime said, throwing her hands up in surrender. "By the way, do you always make assumptions like that when two people of the same sex share a room?"

"No. And you're right. I guess I shouldn't have but—"

"But you assumed we were together because after our kiss all those years ago you figured I turned out to be a lesbian and naturally would have a partner by now. Am I right?"

She nodded, but before she was able to answer Jaime leaned forward and placed a finger over Sierra's lips to silence her.

"You're right. I am a lesbian. But I'm not with anyone. Truthfully, I've never been in a serious relationship."

She wanted to cry. Everything she'd assumed about Jaime was bullshit conjecture. She wanted to fling herself into Jaime's arms and never let go. But Jaime had already admitted that their kiss all those years ago had been a mistake. The thought suddenly made the three cups of coffee she'd already had that morning turn to acid in her stomach. "That's hard to believe. But I'm sure you'll find someone eventually."

"Yeah…maybe."

Jaime sounded sad, and Sierra wondered if she was lonely. "So if you planned this whole thing, I guess I also have you to thank for sticking me at a table with Bo Tyson and his pack of brainless wonders." Jaime grinned, clearly changing the subject.

"Oops." She winced. "Yeah. Sorry about that."

"Forgiven. But why did you do it? You couldn't have forgotten how much I can't stand the jocks and their snooty wives."

"Look, I'm sorry." No way would she tell Jaime she'd done it out of jealousy. At least this problem she could fix. "I'll go talk to someone today and use my powers of travel-agent persuasion to get you a table change. Will that help?"

"That's a sweet offer but let me ask Darlene first. I don't want to assume anything and get on her bad side."

"Ooh, I remember that side," she said, casually touching Jaime's hand. "Tread carefully."

"Always."

They sat quietly for a moment, both of them staring at the way their hands fit together on the tabletop. She gave Jaime a shy smile before looking out the window, unsure what to say or do next, unwilling to break the fragile moment. A group of boisterous men entered the lounge, effectively shattering the calm.

"Well, well," Bo said staring down at Jaime and Sierra. "Seems I was wrong about you, Rivers. Moving on to greener pastures?"

"Bo," Jaime replied.

"Hey, Sierra," he said. "Long time no see."

"You too, Bo. You look well." She automatically slipped into tour-operator mode in an effort to keep things pleasant.

"Of course I do," he said as his friends laughed. "But thanks for noticing."

"What do you want, Tyson?" Jaime said, her voice low and heavy.

"Nothing. Besides, we all know there's nothing you can give me anyway. But Sierra here might have something to offer." Bo placed his hand on her shoulder but she effectively shrugged it off. She wanted him to go away, but he wasn't worth the anger she could see building in Jaime's eyes.

"Don't," Jaime growled, and stood.

"Or what?" he said. "You gonna do something? Please, I can eat your weight in breakfast. Besides, I didn't hear Sierra complaining."

The second time he tried to touch her, Jaime batted his hand away. Thankfully, before things got out of hand, they'd attracted the attention of a crew member who happened to be walking by.

"Excuse me," a tall man in a white uniform asked in a no-nonsense tone. "Can I be of some assistance here?"

"We're fine," Bo said, but his eyes betrayed his anger. "Aren't we, ladies?"

"Perfect. Thanks," Jaime said, standing protectively in front of Sierra. "I think it's time you run along, Tyson. I heard pool ping-pong is at nine sharp. Don't want you jock types to miss out on that action."

Bo backed away, his eyes still locked on Jaime's. "Yeah…right. Come on, guys. Let's leave these nice ladies to their day."

The minute Bo and his friends disappeared and the crewman found something else to occupy his time, her anger got the best of her. They weren't in high school anymore and the déjà vu with the entire situation suddenly made her irritable. "Was all that really necessary?"

"You can't be serious? Sierra, he was being a jerk."

"So what, damn it! He could have hurt you."

"Please. You think I give shit about that? All I care about is that he touched you. Even if he doesn't have the balls to do anything, I won't have him or anyone talking to you that way."

"They're only words, Jaime."

"No, they're not just words!" Jaime said, her frustration obviously getting the best of her. She lowered her voice. "Don't you see? I'm the token lesbian on this fucking cruise. He knew that comment would rile me. I bet he's making assumptions about us this minute because he saw you hanging out with me just like his wife did when she saw Darlene and me together yesterday. I don't want him starting rumors about us, although it's probably too late to stop them."

"Since when are you worried about rumors? There was talk about us being together in school too, but it didn't seem to bother you then."

Jaime straightened as if stunned. "You knew about those?"

"Hell, yes! Who didn't? But I never allowed them to upset me." Her throat went tight as her new reality sank in. Not only did Jaime regret the past, but she also didn't want any speculation regarding their relationship, no matter how innocent it was. The realization stung, but she refused to allow it to interfere with her only chance of rekindling a friendship with Jaime.

"Look, I'm sorry," Jaime said. I guess I shouldn't have let Bo get to me. How about we go enjoy the rest of the morning by taking a walk up on the top deck?"

She agreed even though it saddened her to think that Jaime would never see her as anything more than a friend.

CHAPTER SEVEN

Flynn looked out over the horizon and took in the majestic sunset, something she'd never done throughout all her travels. Not understanding the beauty they held until now, she glanced sideways at the woman who made her see everything in a different light. Alex's chin was tilted toward the darkening sky, her eyes closed. Soft flutters of Alex's golden hair whipped around her face, and when Alex opened her eyes and gazed over at her, Flynn's heart nearly stopped.

"Why do you put up with this job?" Flynn asked, brushing away a few errant strands.

"Of all the people to ask me that question." Alex teased her.

"No, really. I'd like to know why you find your job rewarding?" Flynn grabbed Alex's hand, holding it gently between both of hers. "You show up to meet me for a few minutes here and there, only to return to base until the next mission. There's no adventure involved in that. Surely you don't do it for the money."

Alex wiped at her tear-streaked face. "Maybe I do it because I enjoy it."

"Why don't I believe you?" Flynn asked in barely a whisper.

"Maybe because I never gave you a reason to trust me."

"How can you say that? You who have sent me on countless missions. You who have always been there for me when I returned. I trust no one more." Flynn ached to pull Alex into her arms—to kiss those tears away, but she would never cross that invisible barrier that

Alex always erected between them unless invited. Instead she wiped away a tear with her thumb. "Please, Alex. Tell me the truth."

Flynn had spent her whole life searching for something that she'd never thought she'd find. Was it because she had been looking for it in the wrong places? Was it because she had no clue what she was looking for in the first place? Or was it because she had been too blind to see what was right in front of her all along?

"The truth, Flynn?" Alex rested Flynn's hand over her heart. "Neither of us is ready to face the truth. But I promise if that time comes, I'll answer every question you have."

Jaime drummed her fingers against the desk, barely conscious of Darlene staring at the computer screen over her shoulder. She'd been typing for hours and needed to get her thoughts out before they vanished. Finally Flynn had a path, but she still wasn't certain if this journey would be Flynn's last. What to do—

"When did you start writing again?" Darlene asked.

"Jesus!" She held one hand over her heart while she slammed her laptop shut with the other. "You scared the shit out of me! You know I don't like people reading my stuff before I'm finished."

"I didn't mean to snoop, and I didn't read it. But this is a big deal. Something's driving you to write again, and I think that's wonderful."

She powered down her Mac, moving to sit on the bed opposite Darlene. She too had been questioning her sudden motives for writing, but the words were starting to flow again, and for the moment, that had to be enough.

"I can see the wheels spinning and smoke coming out of your ears. Cool your brain before you explode."

"Easy for you to say. Maybe writing again isn't a good idea."

"Why? It's what you do. Who you are."

"No, it's not. I'm nobody anymore." She stood abruptly, pacing in a tight line.

"If you expect me to sit here and buy that tormented-writer crap you've been spewing for the past few years you can forget it. It's an excuse, plain and simple. Everything has always been in here," she said, stabbing Jaime in the forehead with her finger. "You never needed anything to help you write. It was just easier to believe you did."

"And how do I know that's not crap *you're* spewing?"

"Easy. Because I know you're not taking anything now, and after what I just read…" Darlene placed her hand over her mouth, sporting a "whoops" look.

"You told me you didn't read it."

"Okay." Darlene held her hands up to ward off another tongue-lashing. "I admit I read *some*. And I have to tell you, it was some of your best work."

Jaime plopped backward onto the bed and flung her arm over her eyes. "I don't want to talk about it."

"But is what I read true? Is Flynn really falling in love?"

If Darlene asked one more question Jaime didn't have the answer to, she'd smother her with a pillow. This is why she spent a majority of her time alone. She didn't want to have to answer to anyone or have someone question her writing, especially at its early stages. Until she was happy with her work, she felt exposed in ways she couldn't explain. "What part of 'I don't want to talk about it' don't you get?"

"Whatever. Be a stubborn ass. I need to get dressed."

Jaime gave a frustrated groan. She'd been aggravated since the incident with Sierra and Bo and had no idea how to approach Sierra to fix the tension between them. At the time she thought she'd done the right thing by stepping between them. She'd wanted to protect Sierra. Bo had been staring at Sierra like a bear seeing its first meal after hibernation, and she couldn't stand by while he pawed at her like a piece of meat. The thought of him touching Sierra still irritated her and, looking back, no matter how mad Sierra had been at her, she'd do exactly the same thing again, damn the consequences. But tension had accompanied every step of their walk together, and they had gone their separate ways with an awkward promise to meet for a drink at some point. It sucked.

Maybe it was time for a distraction. Anything to take her mind off Sierra and everyone associated with this trip. Picking up her Kindle, she decided to lose herself in a hot, steamy romance.

Darlene emerged from the bathroom, staring at her oddly. "Aren't you coming to dinner?"

"Uh…no. You can't possibly expect me to sit through another gag fest, especially after what happened last night."

"You know as well as I do that you not wanting to go to dinner has nothing to do with last night."

"The hell it doesn't."

"Bullshit! I heard about this morning. The gossip mill was overactive as usual. Marcy did everything but announce over the ship's loudspeaker what happened with Bo and his dumb-ass friends. Of course, the way Marcy told the story, you pushed her poor husband, and because he's such a gentleman and would never hit a lady, he took the high road and walked away so you wouldn't get in trouble for your 'unprovoked' attack."

"He's a jackass."

"Duh. So what prompted the unusual display of hostility, or do I really have to ask?"

Jaime picked at an imaginary piece of lint on her pants.

"Humph, just what I thought. What did he say to Sierra that made you get physical?"

Just thinking about Bo's insinuating remarks made her want to put her fist through the wall. His first mistake was to make assumptions about Sierra in front of her and expect her to stand by and take it. Regardless of how Jaime felt about her, Sierra was straight, and she wasn't about to let people walk around the ship for the next week making faces and comments about Sierra being her special friend. She'd figured the best thing to do was stay out of the public eye and try to get some writing done.

"I didn't get physical."

"Then tell me what happened."

"Nothing, really. He made some snide comment to Sierra similar to what he said to you at dinner. He touched her and I stepped between them. Luckily, a crew member happened to be walking by and then Bo took off. Sierra pretty much gave me the cold shoulder after that. End of story."

"And that's why you're avoiding dinner."

"I'm not *avoiding* anything. I'm not hungry so go enjoy it without me."

"Fine!"

Darlene stormed out of their room, leaving her to feel guilty about how she'd treated her friend who had always been supportive of her. She burst from the room and raced down the hallway, catching Darlene at the elevator.

"Wait!" she said, skidding to a halt. "I'm sorry. I guess I'm already getting grumpy from being around all these people. If you really want me to go to dinner, I will."

Darlene gave her a quick hug. "No worries. Besides, how can I subject you to another dose of Bo and his friends after that story? I feel bad for you though. I just don't know what to do about it."

"*You* don't have to do anything. As for dinner, I hear the buffet's pretty good."

"I could join you?"

Darlene's offer was sweet but the off-the-shoulder dress she was wearing was meant to show off, not hide. "Nah, you go ahead. Give Bo a big kiss for me."

"Oh, don't worry, pal," Darlene said, an evil glint in her eyes. "I plan to give Bo something tonight and a kiss is far from it."

"Don't get in any trouble," Jaime said as the doors closed.

She made her way back down the hallway to change into a pair of sweats and a T-shirt. Maybe a quick bite to eat was a good idea before she made her way to the ship's gym to work off some excess energy. She needed something to do, anything to keep her busy so she wouldn't feel as empty as the hallway she was standing in.

Sierra picked at her appetizers, knowing why Jaime hadn't appeared for dinner. The empty seat at Bo's table spoke volumes. She'd felt terrible about the way they'd left things and had planned to apologize for her cold behavior the second she spotted Jaime. Unfortunately, since Jaime hadn't made an appearance, it didn't seem she was going to get the chance.

After taking the afternoon to question why she was so angry with Jaime, she concluded it had nothing to do with the incident with Bo and everything to do with the fact that their first kiss obviously didn't mean the same thing to Jaime as it had to her. Rationally, she shouldn't have expected more than just friendly feelings after all this time, but common sense went right out the window where Jaime was concerned. Jaime had made it very clear that she didn't want anyone to mistake them as a couple. That realization had hurt, but she couldn't deny that every time she saw Jaime, her breath caught in her chest and her heart rate kicked into overdrive. Friends, Jaime had said. Could she really be just Jaime's friend? If that was her only option, as painful as the idea seemed, she'd decided that *friends* was better than nothing at all.

Salads had arrived as she spotted Darlene heading in the direction of the restrooms. Since her appetite was long gone, she followed Darlene, hoping to catch her when she exited the restroom.

"Hey," Darlene said, nearly crashing into Sierra. "Need something?"

"Hi…yeah, actually. I was wondering if you can tell me where Jaime is?"

"The buffet, probably. Not sure though."

"Do you know why?"

"Actually, it's because of what happened earlier between you and Bo."

"Did she tell you that?"

"She didn't have to. Marcy did everything but take out an ad in the ship's newsletter."

"The whole ship knows?" Sierra said. She was going to kill Marcy.

"Oh, yeah. And you know Jaime. It's always been easier for her to avoid than engage."

"I remember."

Sierra flashed back to her sophomore year when Riley Crisco, the varsity quarterback, had tried to kiss her on a dare by his friends. Luckily the rumor mill had been overactive that day too, and Jaime had caught wind of it and intervened. For weeks after, Jaime had avoided the cafeteria because she didn't want to have to listen to the entire football team's taunts. Sierra found her every day and made it a point to take her lunch. Even then, Jaime had always stuck up for her.

"I'll go look for her," she said. "Thanks, Darlene."

"You bet."

Darlene disappeared into the dining room as Sierra keyed the elevator to take her to the tenth floor. She would have made a clean getaway if Marcy hadn't staggered up to her to lean heavily with one hand braced against the elevator wall.

"I just don't see it," Marcy slurred.

"See what, Marcy?" She didn't have time for Marcy's crap, especially since it was because of Marcy and her man-child husband that Jaime was upstairs eating alone.

"See why Jaime Rivers has always stood up for you, of course. Obviously she's still attracted to you."

Jaime, attracted to me? Not likely. She's done everything but tell me she wants nothing to do with me beyond friendship.

"What I don't get," Marcy said, "is why you keep making that poor girl suffer? We all know she's a," Marcy looked around as if to make sure no one could hear her and whispered, "you know, a lesbian. Doesn't she understand that she should leave straight girls alone? That scene earlier with protecting your honor and all. Pullleaseee. Did she think you'd switch teams and run into her arms because she stood up to my husband? She's just lucky he's such an upstanding man and didn't seriously injure her."

Apparently Darlene had been right. Everyone had heard about what had happened that morning, and as usual Bo and Marcy were putting their own personal spin on the details. Suddenly her protective instincts kicked in. Here was her chance to add another piece of gossip to the rumor mill. She motioned Marcy closer with her finger.

"Well, maybe that would all be true, Marcy," she whispered, "if I were straight. Good night. "

She brushed past Marcy, hoping that would take some of the heat off Jaime and give Marcy and the rest of her classmates someone else to talk about, if only for the next few hours. She refused to allow Jaime to be the martyr again or have her eat her dinners alone for the rest of the cruise, if she had anything to say about it.

❖

Jaime had never felt so alone. Normally she made good use of her time, but as she sat inside the quiet café and pushed her food around on her plate, the silence was physically painful. She'd barely touched dinner and was intending to check out one of the early comedy shows when Sierra suddenly sat next to her.

"Hi."

"Hi," she said cautiously.

"Want some company?"

She wanted Sierra's company desperately, but after that morning she had no idea where she stood. Being around Sierra was like walking on quicksand. One misstep and she'd be submersed so deep in emotional mud she wasn't sure if she'd survive the undertow. Not able to meet Sierra's gaze she shrugged and studied the untouched plate of food in front of her.

"Jaime, please look at me."

The pleading note in Sierra's voice was enough to catch her attention. Immediately Sierra's hypnotic blue eyes drew her in. She scooted closer but had a hard time not touching Jaime. A very hard time. "You've always had the most beautiful eyes."

"Thank you," Sierra said, and blushed.

"Don't thank me. Thank your parents. I'm sorry if I embarrassed you."

"Are you?"

"Not in the least." She smiled. "I'm surprised though. I figured you'd be used to those types of compliments."

"What makes you think so?"

She tilted her head, studying Sierra closely. "You mean to tell me your husband never compliments you?"

"Husband?" Sierra eyed Jaime curiously. "I'm not married."

She was as confused as Sierra looked. "That's what it said on Facebook last time I checked—"

"Facebook? You checked me out on Facebook?"

She swallowed and looked away. Sierra was going to think she was some kind of creepy stalker or something. This was why she had to tread carefully. So much for caution. She could already feel herself sinking. There had to be a way out. *Think, damn it.* "It was totally an accident. Someone volunteered the information. It's not like I asked or anything."

"Oh, I get it. You didn't care or want to know anything about me."

"No! That's not it at all." She couldn't stand the distance between them any longer. She was saying all the wrong things and needed Sierra to hear her out. Without thinking about the possible consequences, she twined her fingers through Sierra's, surprised at the warmth of Sierra's skin against hers but even more surprised that Sierra didn't pull away. "Sierra, please. I *do* care. Tell me whatever you want. I'm here to listen. Swear."

Sierra paused for a second as if chewing on Jaime's words. "I was married, but only for a short time. It's over."

"What happened?"

"Simple answer is I shouldn't have married him."

"There's a more complicated one?"

"Yes, smart-ass, there is," Sierra said as her expression turned serious.

She squeezed Sierra's hand and could tell by the miserable expression on Sierra's face that there was more to the story, but she wasn't going to push. She swallowed hard, feeling like her next question was probably one of the most important in her life. Her heart beat furiously in her chest. She cleared her throat. "So are you…uh…seeing anyone now?"

"No," Sierra said softly.

That one simple word allowed her to take her first deep breath since boarding the ship. Sierra was unattached, and even though she was straight, they could at least work on forging a new friendship. Feeling as though a hundred-pound weight had been lifted off her chest, she quickly stood and pulled Sierra up with her. "Can I interest you in an ice cream?"

Sierra giggled like a school kid, swinging their joined hands between them. "I'd love one."

"Great, follow me. I know the perfect spot."

Chapter Eight

S ierra vaulted out of bed the following morning, excited about the prospect of a new day and her renewed friendship with Jaime. With only an hour to get ready before going on shore, she took a quick shower and fixed her hair. After deciding a ponytail would be a more suitable hairstyle for the hot weather, she threw on a pair of white shorts and a royal-blue tank top and went to join the other passengers waiting in the stairwell to disembark.

Passengers cluttered the hallway like cattle trapped in a pen, eagerly waiting to make their way off ship to enjoy the Florida sunshine. She self-consciously fidgeted with her shorts, having chosen to wear the shortest pair she owned in an effort to catch Jaime's eye. Now that she knew Jaime was single, she planned to go to any lengths to get Jaime to notice her.

Over an ice-cream sundae last night, it seemed they were able to pick up right where they left off all those years ago. Minus the kiss, of course. If friendship was the only thing on the menu, she would make the most of it. But if there was any chance in hell of something else, she planned to try for it.

For over two hours, they'd shared stories, talked about the old days, and walked on the upper deck overlooking the entire ship. They fell into easy conversation, and when Jaime offered to spend the next day with her sightseeing, she accepted immediately. Since neither one of them had booked one of the many excursions offered by the cruise line, they decided to explore Key West on their own and maybe book some type of tour once they stepped onto land. No matter. She didn't care what they did as long as she was able to spend time with Jaime.

Ten minutes later, she emerged from the ship and found Jaime leaning against the deck railing closest to the large Welcome to the Florida Keys sign. If a person didn't know Jaime, she would have appeared relaxed, but Sierra picked up on Jaime's anxiety the minute she spotted her. Jaime's furrowed brow and hands tucked deep into her cargo-short pockets meant she was trying her best to hide her angst. Deciding it was probably due to the large crowd congregating on the pier, she swooped in for a rescue.

"Hi," she said as Jaime pushed away from the railing.

Jaime stared at her and grinned, mischief sparkling in her eyes. "Hey, yourself. Nice shorts."

"Thanks." Heat rose in her cheeks that had nothing to do with the soaring temperature. "Glad you like them."

"Very much. You all set?"

"Yep, but how about a picture before we head out?"

"Sure."

They stuck their heads through two cardboard floatation devices and smiled big for the camera before heading in the direction of Key West's historic Seaport Boardwalk. They'd planned to do some mindless window-shopping, but Jaime stopped short when someone approached them about kayaking trips.

"How about it?" Jaime asked.

"How about what?"

"Kayaking. Sounds like fun. Let's do it. My treat."

She stared at Jaime like she'd lost her mind. "Are you *crazy*?"

"Sometimes, yeah. But I don't see what that has to do with anything."

"Everything, if you think I'm going to get into that needle-thin piece of plastic that looks like it could tip over any second. If you remember correctly, I don't like boats. It took me months to swallow the idea of going on a boat that size," she said, pointing to their luxury liner.

"That's not a boat, it's a ship."

"Semantics, smart-ass. It floats on the damn water, and it could sink. No way."

"Oh, come on. It'll be fun. Just think, your life will be in my hands."

She shuddered. Jaime's hands, long-fingered and full of strength. She couldn't think about them in any capacity, not without her palms sweating and her heart racing out of control like a runaway train. Why did she suddenly forget how to breathe?

"Sierra, you okay?"

"Fine, yeah, sorry. Where were we?" *Because I was thinking of your hands and how if they touched me—Stop!* "Oh yeah, I remember. You want me to crawl into that mini-torpedo thingy over there, and I was thinking about all the possible horrific things that could go wrong."

"Nothing's going to go wrong. I'll protect you. Scout's honor."

"You weren't a scout."

"Now who's being the smart-ass?" Jaime teased her. "Please?"

"Oh, God! Begging. Really?"

"Is it working?" Jaime smiled in that way she would never be able to resist.

"Okay, okay." What a sucker she was. No way could she say no when Jaime used that sad, pathetic look that would make a golden retriever proud. "I'm game. But if I do this, we have to make a deal."

Jaime nodded her head warily.

"I'll promise to get into that nonexistent piece of plastic with you if you promise to take me snorkeling when we get to St. Lucia on Thursday. I've always wanted to snorkel, and the ocean where we grew up was murky and too damn cold. What do you say?"

Suddenly Jaime paled and broke into a sweat. The fun-loving Jaime from a second ago disappeared and in her place was the nervous, unsure Jaime who had been waiting for her when she first exited the ship. The transformation was immediate and startling. Jaime grasped blindly for something to hold onto and ended up reaching for her.

She wrapped her arms around Jaime's shoulders and pulled her close. "Hey, hey. What is it? What's wrong?"

"I can't. I can't. I'm so sorry, I can't," Jaime said in a pained whisper. She threw her hands over her face, obviously in an effort to hide her humiliation.

"Shh…calm down. It's okay. Whatever it is, we'll fix it." She held Jaime tight until her trembling body quieted to a few slow, shaky breaths. "What's scaring you?"

"I can't go into the water."

She would have believed almost anything except that. Jaime's confession didn't make sense. Jaime had been a competitive surfer when she was a teenager and had spent countless hours in or near the water. She recalled even making a joke about Jaime being part dolphin when she was a teenager. "Sweetie," she said, stroking Jaime's sweat-soaked hair. "I want to help, really. But you're going to have to give me more to go on than that."

Jaime disentangled herself from her and stared out at the vast ocean. Whatever was troubling her was too painful to voice. The thought of Jaime in any type of pain made her want to pull her back into her arms and shield her from any type of suffering again. As Jaime white-knuckled the railing, she wanted to touch Jaime, but she also didn't want to spook her anymore than she already was.

"I want to tell you," Jaime said, turning toward her. "I just can't. Not yet."

Not being able to handle the tormented look on Jaime's face any longer, she opened her arms to give Jaime the option, just like Jaime had given her the first night on the ship. Without hesitation, Jaime leaned forward and wrapped her arms around Sierra's neck, hugging her close.

"You can tell me whenever you want," she whispered into Jaime's ear. "I'm here and I won't push."

"Thanks." Jaime pulled back and wiped at her eyes. "It's not that I don't want to. I'm just not used to talking about it with anyone. I'd really like to go snorkeling with you. Please believe me. I just don't know if I can."

"That's okay. It was only a suggestion." She grasped Jaime's hand and the trembling fingers squeezed back. "Besides, we have days to think about it. We don't have to do anything you don't want to. But if you decide to go, I'll be with you the entire way."

Jaime inhaled sharply and tightened her grip, obviously needing someone to steady her through whatever storm raged inside her. Thankfully Sierra was willing to be her anchor. "Okay, I'll think about it."

"Good. Jaime, do you trust me?" She held her breath. She needed Jaime to say yes. She needed Jaime to understand that no matter what, she'd always be there for her.

"I do. Swear."

Swear. That's the second time in two days Jaime had used that word. Until yesterday, she hadn't had anyone say that to her in ten years. Only Jaime ever used the word *swear* with so much conviction, and she only said it when she was being absolutely serious. She released her breath. "Then I promise, nothing's going to happen to you."

"I believe you."

"You'd better. So, what's this nonsense about kayaking?"

❖

Jaime maneuvered the kayak back to shore, holding the small craft steady for Sierra to disembark. The last two hours had flown by in a mixture of laughter and childish bantering, and the rush of adrenaline coursing through her veins had nothing to do with the kayaking trip and everything to do with her feisty boatmate.

Sierra had sat in front of her, making fun of her steering ability and yelling at her when she thought they were going to topple the boat. Obviously Sierra's sense of humor was her way of coping with her fear. After a short time, Sierra had relaxed and seemed satisfied with Jaime's control of the small vessel. She had almost forgotten how much fun it was to joke with Sierra, and in no time, they had begun teasing each other like they had when they were younger. What pleased her most was that every time Sierra peeked over her shoulder, Sierra threw her a smile that penetrated her heart.

"So what do you think?" she asked, handing Sierra the paddles.

"You didn't drown us. That counts for something, right?"

"And you call me a smart-ass."

Sierra laughed but stopped her with a hand on her arm as she crawled out of the small craft. "No, seriously. I had a great time. Thank you."

"Really? You mean you'd do it again?"

"Don't push your luck, Rivers," Sierra said, grabbing one end of the boat to help her lift it out of the water.

They headed back to the ship after they returned the kayak. Before going to their rooms, Jaime planned to ask Sierra if she wanted to catch an early show later but was surprised when Sierra stopped her with a hand on her arm.

Sierra had touched her on and off all day, but she chalked the contact up to the normal social graces between two friends. This touch was different. Her skin prickled with nervous energy and she was sure Sierra felt it too. The simple touches had been driving her crazy all day. She fought every instinct not to pull Sierra into her arms, to constantly remind herself that Sierra was straight. The last time she forgot that fact, Sierra had walked out on her and they'd lost ten precious years. No way would she make that same mistake again. "Did you forget something?"

"Actually, yes. I wanted to ask you if you were planning to attend formal night tonight?"

"Formal night?" She silently berated herself for not paying more attention to Darlene when she'd rambled on about the ship's activities.

Sierra shook her head in obvious disbelief. "I should have known you wouldn't have any idea about one of the largest social gatherings on the ship. You know, we get dressed up nicely for dinner and then we dance and have drinks. Kind of like prom for mature people."

The last thing she wanted to do was parade around in a monkey suit with thousands of people, but the look of hope in Sierra's eyes caused her to cave immediately. She really wanted to spend the evening with Sierra because the prospect of being alone the rest of the evening suddenly seemed unappealing. "Sounds like fun."

"Really, you'll go?"

"Sure. What do I have to do?"

"You're incorrigible. What am I gonna do with you?"

She could think of a thousand things, none of them having to do with dinner. "Sorry, my social graces are subpar."

Sierra laughed. "No worries. Gives me something to work on. Tell you what. Meet me at the bottom of the main staircase, say, seven thirty. I'll take care of the rest. Deal?"

"It's a date. I mean…"

"Perfect," Sierra said, backing away shyly. "See you then."

She waited for Sierra to disappear into the elevator before panic set in. She needed to find Darlene quick and tell her what was going on before the rest of her evening turned into a total disaster. *Prom for mature people? What the hell am I doing?*

Jaime paced the confines of her tiny room, trying to decide what to wear to what the ship called the Captain's Formal Dinner Night. She hadn't planned to play dress-up, and as she stared at the casual clothes in her closet, she began to hyperventilate.

As her pacing speed increased so did her heart rate. She clenched and unclenched her fists, trying to think up an excuse, any excuse that could get her out of this dinner without hurting Sierra's feelings. *Maybe I can tell her that I'm not feeling well?* "Of course you can't lie to her, stupid," she said to the empty room.

"Lie to who?" Darlene said, bursting into the cabin. "And you know you couldn't lie to your reflection, so whatever your plan is— forget it."

She was so happy to see Darlene she flung her arms around her neck. "Jesus, I'm glad you're here. You'll never believe what I've done."

"Whoa! Back up, stud. I'm taken," Darlene said, shooing her away.

"You wish." Jaime guffawed. "But seriously. I have so fucked up this time."

"What did you do now? Push someone overboard?"

"Worse! I promised Sierra that I would go to this stupid captain's thing tonight, but I don't have anything to wear. Look at what I brought with me." She ripped all her clothes out of the closet and tossed them on the floor. "I'm screwed!"

"Oh, is that all?" Darlene picked up the phone. "It's a go," she said into the receiver before putting the phone down.

"What the hell does that mean?"

"You'll see."

Five minutes later, she was still quizzing Darlene about her mysterious phone conversation when a knock sounded on their door. A handsome European gentleman strode into the room and placed a garment bag onto her bed, leaving after receiving a tip and a thank-you from Darlene in French.

"Well, you gonna stand there with that dumb look on your face or are you going to open it?"

She pulled back the zipper and stared at the contents in disbelief. Running her hand down the shiny black lapels, she asked, "Where did you get this?"

"The tuxedo shop downstairs. I knew after you ran into Sierra yesterday and spent all day with her today, she'd want you to go to dinner with her tonight. So this afternoon I took the liberty of ordering it for you. It should fit perfectly."

"Wow, you're a lifesaver. But you know this isn't a date, right?"

"Of course it's a date. She asked you to go, didn't she?"

"Well, yeah but..." They'd had a great day but Sierra was straight. Bingo! Question answered. "Come on, Darlene, be serious. She's straight. It's just a friend thing, you know?"

"Whatever. You can be so dense sometimes. But honestly, I think it's kinda cute."

"Darlene!"

"Okay, okay. No more teasing. But think about what you're saying. You just told me it was her idea."

"I...well..."

"Like I said. Dense. Come on, get dressed, hot stuff. You don't want to keep the lady waiting."

She grabbed Darlene and hugged her tight. "Thanks. I owe you."

"Damn right you do." Darlene squeezed back, then shoved her playfully away. "And quit already with all the hugging or I'm going to start taking this 'it's a friend thing' the wrong way."

"Dream on."

She quickly planted a kiss on Darlene's cheek and ducked into the bathroom before Darlene could swat her. She had less than an hour to shower and get dressed for dinner, and she planned to look her best. If she couldn't have Sierra, she'd show her what she was missing.

CHAPTER NINE

Jaime adjusted the collar on her crisp black tuxedo jacket, feeling a little overdressed. As Darlene had predicted, the tuxedo with its sleek lines and perfectly fitted shoulders appeared to have been designed especially for her. She'd have to remember to buy something for Darlene on shore tomorrow, a little gift to thank her for helping make her dinner with Sierra as perfect as possible. As she entered the Promenade Deck, her anxiety dissipated. Monkey suits everywhere. At least she wouldn't be the only one uncomfortable tonight.

Hundreds of people roamed around looking as though they were going to a ball instead of sitting down to dinner. Fancy gowns and tuxedos of all colors peppered the landscape, and she descended the spiral staircase scanning anxiously for Sierra, unable to locate her among the mass of people. Photo booths were scattered along three decks as dozens of couples waited in line to get their souvenir picture taken. She decided to sit in one of the lobby chairs, swiveling back and forth in nervous anticipation. The hair on her neck prickled as she felt someone watching her. Glancing skyward she gasped audibly.

Sierra made her way down the red carpeted steps and Jaime stood slowly, taking in every luscious curve, every bare inch of skin left exposed by the red strapless gown that hugged her body like... Jaime was momentarily paralyzed.

"Do you like?" Sierra asked.

She nodded, speechless, her knees threatening to give out at the beauty before her. Sierra laughed in obvious pleasure.

"Come on, handsome. Escort me to the dining room."

Sierra weaved her arm through Jaime's as they stopped to take a picture before entering the elegant dining hall. Two people at Sierra's table had cancelled the trip at the last minute, and Sierra invited Darlene and Jaime to sit with her instead of with their own awful tablemates. Everyone seemed relieved by the arrangement, Jaime more than anyone.

Mozart's *Eine Kleine Nachtmusik* radiated from the ship's speakers as guests murmured in appreciation over Maine lobster and Baked Alaska. Jaime rarely took her eyes off Sierra, more than proud to be sitting next to the most stunning woman in the room. Sierra glowed. Her flawless skin became even more vibrant when someone said something to make her laugh. Every time Sierra turned to speak with her, it took all of her willpower to keep her eyes above Sierra's cleavage. Considering she was taller than Sierra, even when seated, it took great restraint since she had an unobstructed view of two of the most perfect breasts she had ever seen. Damn, Sierra could turn her on without even trying.

All evening long, Sierra innocently touched her on the arm or leaned close to hear what she was saying over the noise of the crowd. When she asked Sierra if she liked her dessert, Sierra leaned forward and placed her hand high on Jaime's thigh. If Sierra only knew how hard she worked to stifle a groan, that another few inches higher and she would most likely embarrass herself by moaning out loud. Normally women didn't hold this type of power over her. She ached with every caress, her nerves bowstring-tight every time Sierra leaned close to her.

Darlene politely excused herself and joined a group of fellow classmates for an after-dinner drink, leaving her and Sierra alone at the table. They had finished dessert but she couldn't bear for the night to end.

"Would you like to take a walk?" she asked, rising and offering her hand to Sierra.

"Yes." Sierra accepted it. "I'd enjoy that very much."

They strolled along the Royal Promenade, littered with guests taking their time to admire the quaint shops that lined one of the busiest parts of the ship. Combined with restaurants and a few bars, it reminded Jaime of an old-world Italian village with its Tuscan feel and convenient outdoor seating. She pointed to the balconies located above their heads, watching as the other passengers sipped their after-dinner drinks.

They stopped at a champagne bar and sat across from a young couple holding hands and laughing at something the bartender was saying. Sierra ordered a margarita. She ordered a Diet Coke.

"Don't drink?" Sierra asked curiously.

She shrugged. "No, not really my thing."

"Is it the taste you don't like?"

For the second time that day, she hid a part of herself from Sierra. She wouldn't go into detail about her accident, and now she refused to talk about her addiction. How could she tell Sierra that she'd love to have a drink, that drinking was one of the ways she used to cope in social situations? Even though alcohol wasn't the type of drug she preferred, it always helped her get through the awkwardness of the moment. Kind of like this one. She finally responded to Sierra's question. "Among other things."

Sierra shoved away from the bar when a popular nineties tune began to play at a crowded bar next door, clearly letting the subject drop. "Well, then how about dancing? Is that your thing?"

"Uh…dancing? You do mean fast songs, right? Because after watching you dance with Roy Fields at prom, I can't possibly watch you dance slowly with a guy again." *I can't believe I just said that!*

"Fast, slow, whatever," Sierra said, sounding pleased as she playfully tugged on Jaime's hand. "I love this song. Come on."

The bar was packed as dozens of bodies crammed onto the small, circular dance floor. Jaime became immediately aware of a few men scoping out Sierra, recognizing the hungry looks of the dateless few. She held back a scowl, fighting the urge to bare her teeth like a dog protecting its prized bone. Her insides ran cold and a surge of jealousy shot through her. She wanted to assert her right to Sierra, to pull Sierra into her arms and let everyone in that room know that she was off limits. But she didn't have that right. Sierra belonged to no one, especially her. The thought left her feeling helpless. Her anxiety flared. The cramped room closed in around her. But when Sierra turned and looked at her, giving her one of those megawatt smiles, everyone else in the room disappeared until there was only Sierra.

"Come on, I don't bite," Sierra whispered.

The music blared through the speakers as Sierra twirled around her and laughed. She remained rooted to one spot, shifting her weight from foot to foot in a poor semblance of rhythm. Sierra's hands were everywhere. One minute on Jaime's hips, the next up and down her back. Every touch was sweet, sweet torture, and just when she was beginning to loosen up a bit and move more freely to the tempo of the music, the beat changed and the lights dimmed.

Suddenly, a slow, familiar melody began to play and couples moved into each other's arms. She stood motionless, wanting nothing more than to pull Sierra close but fearing her reaction.

Glancing into Sierra's eyes, she inhaled sharply. Sierra's shy smile made her heart hammer. With any other woman, she would have thought the look in Sierra's eyes was desire. She knew better, but damn she was so beautiful, so sexy. Should she take the chance and make the first move, or should she wait to see if Sierra approached her first? Not wanting to waste any more precious moments, she cautiously opened her outstretched hand. Every nerve in her body hummed with tension. Seconds felt like an eternity. She held her breath in anticipation as Sierra stepped closer. But instead of taking her hand, Sierra threw her arms around her neck.

She wanted to cry as Sierra hugged her close. She buried her head in Sierra's shoulder, moving them around the dance floor as if they were one body. Her worry abated and she didn't care about the dozens of eyes that watched them. For the first time in her life, it didn't matter that she was on display. Sierra did that to her—made her do and want things she'd never considered before. It had been that way since they'd first met but had never felt quite so good. Her only hope was that the dance could go on forever, but as she tightened her hold around Sierra's waist, someone tapped her on the shoulder from behind.

"Hey, Jaime—Sierra. Could I cut in?" Paul Bellamy, one of their former classmates asked, extending his hand to Sierra.

She would rather die than let Sierra go, but Sierra hadn't said no. In fact, she hadn't said anything. Taking Sierra's silence for acceptance she nodded, releasing Sierra graciously, even though she felt anything but genial. "No problem, Paul. You two have fun."

Paul took Sierra into his arms as she moved to stand against the bar. Normally, she tried to stay far away from temptation. The bar reeked of alcohol, and at one time she would have wanted to succumb to its powerful effects. Watching Sierra in someone else's arms was pushing her control to the limit. One drink wouldn't stop the pain, but it could sure dull the hell out of it. Fighting her inner demons, she closed her eyes and recited the Serenity Prayer. She'd memorized it after her first meeting, and even though she wasn't necessarily a religious person, every time she said the words she was back in that room struggling through her first night of sobriety. The familiar chant reminded her that no matter how hard she thought it was to go on, it was even tougher to go back.

Sierra moved in time with Paul but had no idea what the hell had just happened. One minute she was dancing with Jaime and it was as if all her dreams were finally coming true. The next she was dancing with a former classmate who smelled of Old Spice aftershave and stale beer while Jaime stood staring at her from the opposite end of the room.

Paul Bellamy was one of those all-around great guys. Even so, the last thing she wanted to do was dance with him instead of stay wrapped up in Jaime's arms. Her temper simmered below the surface. It wasn't Paul's fault. He had no idea he'd interrupted a private moment. What made her angry was that Jaime had no problem handing her off like the entire night had meant nothing to her.

Unable to keep her anger in check any longer, she politely excused herself and stalked to the bar. She couldn't read the expression on Jaime's face but had had enough of trying to figure her out. "Why did you leave?"

"He asked you to dance," Jaime said flatly, her words matching the barren look in her eyes. "What was I supposed to say, no?"

"Yes." She grabbed Jaime by the hand and yanked her out of the bar. She didn't want to have this conversation in front of a bunch of people, and she knew Jaime had never been big on crowds.

"Sierra? What the hell?" Jaime planted her feet, bringing them both to a stop in front of the elevators. She didn't reply but instead pushed Jaime into the elevator the minute the doors opened. "What are you—"

"Shut up."

"Excuse me?"

"There is no excuse for you." She closed the distance between them, grabbing Jaime by the lapels. "Now tell me why you left?"

Jaime started to speak but stopped, staring at her mouth. Sierra licked her lips like a lioness on the hunt.

"God damn it, say something."

"You were...dancing. Having fun. I didn't want to get in the way."

"You're so clueless sometimes," she whispered in Jaime's ear, nipping her earlobe. "Don't you see? I didn't want him."

"Then what do you want?" Jaime shivered when she traced a line across her jaw.

"I wanted *you* to dance with me. Only you."

Jaime groaned. That one finger tracing her collarbone was melting away the last vestiges of her restraint. She couldn't think. All she could do was feel. "Oh, God." She groaned again. "You gotta stop. You have no idea what you're doing."

"Really." Sierra leaned closer, resting the front of her body against hers. "I take it back. You're not clueless, just blind."

The soft meeting of lips was nothing like the first kiss they'd shared all those years ago. The possessive way Sierra's lips met Jaime's was very different from the shy, tentative kiss they shared in high school. Sierra darted her tongue slowly in and out between her lips as if daring Jaime to chase her. She moaned and accepted the challenge, deepening the kiss as she pulled Sierra against her, their bodies melding together.

When lack of oxygen forced them apart, she placed her hands on Sierra's shoulders, putting a little distance between them so she could think. Her heart was pounding in her ears, and she was dizzy, probably because all the blood had rushed between her legs. "I didn't know."

"Well, you were always a little slow." Sierra teased her, pulling her closer again. "Now stop talking and do that again."

They managed another brief kiss before the elevators signaled that they had reached the top. Neither one moved. Neither one wanted to.

"Now what?" she said breathlessly. "We could—"

"Yes."

She smiled. "You don't even know what I was going to say."

"I don't care," Sierra said, dragging her out of the elevator by the hand before the doors closed. "As long as it involves only you and me, my answer is yes."

CHAPTER TEN

J aime, this view is breathtaking," Sierra said as Jaime
stood behind her, bracing her arms on the deck railing. In
her strapless dress, she should have thought the cool night air felt
like ice spears piercing her skin, but as she stood between Jaime's
outstretched arms, she felt as though she were standing on a tropical
beach soaking up the afternoon sun. "I feel like I'm flying."

"Uh-oh," Jaime said, snuggling closer. "You're not going to
open your arms and scream 'I'm the king of the world,' right?"

"No, smart-ass, I'm not. Because that would mean in a few
hours the boat would sink. And if that happens, I'm going to kill
you."

"Ooh, I think I'm going to like you getting physical."

Jaime nuzzled Sierra's neck as Sierra leaned her head back,
offering her better access. She turned in Jaime's arms and wrapped
her arms around Jaime's waist. Jaime felt so good, so perfect. "I'm
hoping so since you've never experienced 'physical' with me yet.
But believe me, I'm leaving my options open."

"I like the sound of that."

"So do I." Jaime moved in for a kiss. They took their time
exploring one another, playing a game of cat and mouse. One would
slip her tongue past the other's lips. The other would lean forward
to chase it. The game went on until Sierra slid one of her thighs
between her legs and she pulled back with a groan. Although they
were alone on the deck, someone could come out at any minute, and

she didn't want to create a display, even though she wanted to rip the dress from Sierra's body.

"Whoa, time-out," she said, putting a little distance between them. "I'm losing my grip here."

"Is that a bad thing?" Sierra pulled back, moving her leg away from Jaime's heat. "Besides, I've got you."

"You've pretty much always had me." Jaime wrapped her arms firmly around Sierra and pulled her closer. "Is this okay?"

"It's nice," she said, still not believing that after all this time she was in Jaime's arms. "But to be honest, I think we can make it perfect." They kissed slowly, acquainting themselves thoroughly with each gentle caress of lips and tongue. She could feel the passion pouring from Jaime's body, and when they broke apart, they were both gasping. "Oh my God. If I knew you could kiss like that I'd never have let you out of my sight."

"I've dreamt about kissing you like that since I was fourteen years old. It kept me up late most nights."

Tears misted her eyes. "Jaime, I'm so sorry. All those years wasted. I…"

She buried her head into Jaime's chest and gripped Jaime's jacket hard, afraid she'd somehow slip away. What the hell could she possibly say after all this time that would make any damn bit of difference? She wanted to tell Jaime that she'd been a fool, that she should have never been so quick to judge Jaime's actions. How would Jaime ever trust her again?

"Hey, hey." Jaime tilted her chin up with two fingers as she tried to avoid her eyes. "Stop that. Look at me." When she finally did, Jaime kissed her sweetly. "I've spent too many years missing you. No more dwelling in the past."

"I missed you too. But I still have so many things to tell you."

"I know. We have a lot of catching up to do. I should tell you some things too, but tonight, no more talking. Tonight, I only want to think about having you in my arms. I want to remember every sensation of what kissing you does to me. I want to remember us like this."

She couldn't stop the tears from falling. "You should have been a poet, not a novelist."

"Funny. Some would argue they're one and the same."

"Jaime?"

"What?"

"Shut up."

She pinned Jaime against the railing, placing one of her thighs between Jaime's legs. She nibbled along Jaime's jaw, running both of her palms up the front of Jaime's tuxedo shirt.

"You don't play fair." Jaime moaned, thrusting her hips forward.

She traced her tongue along Jaime's lips, loving the guttural sounds coming from her. She put that heaviness in Jaime's voice and that lazy look on her face, and she'd never felt more powerful. "Since when did you know me ever to play fair?"

Jaime's hands brushed up and down her back as she snaked her hands under Jaime's shirt to do the same. Suddenly, Jaime grabbed her hands, pulling them from underneath her shirt and holding them away from her.

"Something wrong?"

"No," Jaime said quickly. "Everything's fine. But we need to stop."

Jaime stared at her hands, seemingly lost in thought. For the second time that day Jaime had instituted her Jekyll-and-Hyde routine. One minute, Sierra was in the arms of the self-assured Jaime who had kissed her senseless and with abandon. The next minute the person in her arms trembled and looked downright frightened.

"Something I did or said?" she asked.

"No, you're perfect. Honest. But it's been a revealing day for both of us. I think it's best if we slow down. Besides, it's getting kind of warm out here, if you know what I mean."

She wasn't sure about the sudden change in Jaime's behavior, but she knew from past experience that the more she pushed Jaime, the more she'd withdraw. Jaime had already expressed her feelings about others assuming things about their relationship. Could that be why Jaime was slamming on the brakes? "I see."

"Do you?"

Be honest. She needs to know she can trust you. "No. I guess I don't. But I don't want to push you into doing something you don't want to do."

"Don't want..." A flash of disbelief streaked across Jaime's face before she scooped Sierra into her arms and kissed her soundly. "Let's get one thing straight, right now. I want you more than air to breathe. I have since the first day I met you. But look around. We're kind of on display here. Not that I care about what others think, but the things I want to do to you might get us arrested. Besides, I don't want something to happen between us until you know everything about me," she said, her voice tinged with sadness and regret. "I'm not the same person I was ten years ago."

"Oh, sweetie, you *are* the same person, and a whole lot more. I can't imagine what's causing the pain I see in your eyes, but when you're ready to talk about it, I'll be there to listen."

Jaime rested her chin on top of Sierra's head and exhaled deeply. "Thank you."

"You're welcome. Now, enough with all this serious talk for one night. Someone still owes me a dance, and I intend to cash in."

Jaime took her hand and kissed her knuckles. "I'm warning you, dancing isn't one of my strong suits."

"I don't believe that. I'm sure I read somewhere recently that Flynn can tear up the dance floor."

Jaime looked at her in surprise as her cheeks reddened. "Yeah, well, I'm not Flynn."

"You think so, huh? Well, I'm no expert, but do you want to know a secret?"

Jaime nodded, her eyes locked on Sierra's lips.

"I'd take you over her any day."

"Why?"

She studied Jaime, understanding in that moment how truly vulnerable Jaime could be. Jaime's perplexity over why she would choose her over a character in one of her books astounded her, but in actuality, it really shouldn't have been that much of a surprise. Jaime always did underestimate herself, never able to see what others always saw. Jaime was a beautiful person, inside and out. Maybe it was time Sierra showed her. Grabbing Jaime's face with both hands, she stared deeply into Jaime's troubled eyes and said, "Because in all my stories, *you,* Jaime Rivers, are my hero."

The look of shock on Jaime's face when she kissed and released her was priceless. She laughed, pulling Jaime by the hand as they headed toward the lounge. She couldn't remember ever being happier.

❖

Jaime entered the dark bedroom and flipped on the bedside light, startled to find Darlene sitting cross-legged on her bed with a shit-eating grin on her face. "Jesus!" she said, holding a hand over her heart. "You need to stop scaring the crap out of me. My heart can only take so much."

"I'm taking it that means it *did* get a workout?" Darlene asked hopefully.

"Ah." She blushed. "That would be a yes."

"Woo-hoo! Fist bump," Darlene said excitedly, striking her knuckles against Jaime's. "So my meddling worked?"

She smiled. "Yes, it did. Thanks for helping make it special."

"You're welcome. Now spill, because waiting until tomorrow for details is *so* not going to happen."

She shook her head and sat on her bed. She should have known. "What do you want to know?"

"Everything…duh. Let's start with what you two did after dinner."

"Nothing, really." She hoped if she played it casual Darlene would back off with the interrogation. Truth was, she didn't want to talk. She was still coming down off the high of having Sierra in her arms and that was all she wanted to think about, at least until she met up with her the next morning. She didn't want to dim the feelings with words.

"You're never getting to bed at this rate. Come on."

"We danced."

"And…"

Shit. So much for casual. "Okay, okay. We kissed. Happy?"

"Holy shit!" Darlene bounced up and down on the bed. "I knew it! Details, woman."

Hell no, Darlene wasn't getting details. Details would require explaining about Sierra's lips. God, could her lips have been any more sensuous? Then there was Sierra's scent—red wine with a hint of vanilla and cherry blossoms. She was intoxicating, better than any drug Jaime had come across. "Not going to happen," she said, slipping on a pair of boxers and a T-shirt. "You kiss your husband all the time. Figure it out."

"Oh no, you don't," Darlene said as she slipped into her own bed. "I didn't lose three hours of beauty sleep for you to tell me that I can imagine a kiss. There's more, and you're going to lose much more sleep than that if you don't start talking."

"Nothing to say. Maybe if you sleep in tomorrow, you can catch up. Night."

She switched off the light, hoping that in her dreams she could relive those special moments again with Sierra. She turned to face the wall just as a pillow smacked her on top of the head.

"Hey!"

"Hay is for horses." Darlene hit her again. "I warned you."

"Christ, woman." She switched the light back on, finding Darlene standing over her poised to strike again. "I'm curious. Do you use these same torture tactics with your husband?"

"No." Darlene put the pillow down. "If I want information out of him, I torture him with sex. Works like a charm."

"Whoa! TMI. Let's forget I asked."

"Forgotten. I want to hear about you."

"There's really not much to tell. Honest. She confessed she has feelings for me and we kissed. That's all."

"*She* told *you*?"

"Yes."

"Wow." Darlene lowered the pillow. "And you didn't sleep with her?"

"Darlene!"

"Oh, please. Enough with the high-and-mighty routine. You're not that noble. Tell me you didn't want to and I'll let you go to sleep."

"You'll let me?" Darlene lifted the pillow above her head again to prove her point. "Stop, stop." She held her hands up in surrender. "I confess. I wanted to. But…I can't. Not yet."

"What's holding you back?" Darlene asked, serious now.

"What do you think?" She threw off the covers, climbed out of bed, and paced the room. "Don't you get it? She's special. Always has been, always will be. She has no idea about my past. What do you think is going to happen when I tell her about the accident? About rehab. About *everything*."

"Jaime," Darlene said, using that soothing mom tone that she always used to try to calm her. "How do you know until you give her a chance? Maybe she'll surprise you."

She wanted to think that was the case, but where Sierra was concerned she wanted to take things one step at a time.

"Time will tell, won't it?" Too irritated to sleep, she threw on a pair of sweatpants and grabbed her ship's card.

"Now where are you going?"

"For a walk. Don't wait up."

"Jaime, wait!" She paused with her hand poised on the door. "Don't leave. I promise no more prying. You know me, I can't help myself sometimes. I just know how much she means to you. And I want to see you happy again. That's all."

She walked back to Darlene's bed and kissed her on the forehead. "I know you do and I love you for it. Now get some sleep and I'll be back soon. Promise."

She headed for the elevators, hoping that a walk and some sea air would help her clear her head. Sierra had called her a hero, and if she wanted to live up to that standard she'd have to find a way to tell Sierra everything. Heroes didn't hide behind their fear, and neither would she.

Chapter Eleven

Sierra knocked on Jaime's door at eight the next morning, hoping to surprise her with an excursion on the island of Jamaica. Thanks to a last-minute cancellation, she was able to purchase two tickets for one of the most popular vacation destinations on the island. The ship was due to dock in the next few minutes, but after she knocked for the third time on Jaime's door with no answer, she grew apprehensive.

Things had gone better than expected the night before so she'd been surprised when Jaime didn't show up at breakfast after they planned to meet at seven thirty. Sure, Jaime seemed a little nervous at first, but as the evening wore on, her anxiety diminished to the point where she couldn't seem to keep her hands off her. Once they'd parted, after some serious making out, she had spent the rest of the night tossing and turning. All she could think about was how it felt wrapped in Jaime's arms, the way the world disappeared and it was just the two of them. She'd almost begged Jaime to take her back to her room and finish what they'd started on the deck, but Jaime had asked to slow things down. She still wasn't sure why, but she planned to get to the bottom of that mystery today.

By the time she reached Jaime's stateroom door, the constant ache between her legs since last night had turned into a fist of pounding need. Just thinking about being naked in Jaime's arms or succumbing to Jaime's touch made her legs weak, and she had to grab a railing for support. She craved to have Jaime on her, in her, all over her, everywhere. But whatever had been bothering Jaime was getting in the way of fulfilling those needs. If Jaime was anything like she'd been when she was a teenager, Sierra would need a crowbar to pry the information out of her. Regardless, she vowed to take whatever steps necessary to get Jaime to open up.

She had raised her hand to knock one more time when the door flew open and a half-asleep Jaime stood unsteadily in the doorway. Her short hair stuck out in all directions. A red streak slashed across her left cheek, evidence that she'd slept on her arm overnight. She was adorable.

"Hey."

"Hey, sleepyhead. You missed breakfast."

Jaime leaned in for a quick kiss, the simple gesture alleviating all of her earlier doubts. "Sorry, overslept. What time is it?"

"Time to wake up. I have a surprise for you."

"Cool. I love surprises. Can I have it now?"

"Yep. But you have to let me in first." She tried to scoot past Jaime, but Jaime had both arms braced against the doorframe and was expertly blocking her from entering.

"Sorry, but no can do."

"Why not?"

She glanced past Jaime, not noticing Darlene or anyone else in the room with her. Jaime's response didn't make sense, unless she'd been right earlier. Maybe Jaime wasn't looking for more. She had no ties to her other than a few kisses. Okay, maybe they weren't just kisses. Those full-blown make-out sessions still made her wet just thinking about them. Still, what if she'd been wrong about how things were going between them? What if whatever secret Jaime was guarding was too sacred to share with her? Her ex-husband had loads of secrets and look how that relationship had ended. Maybe Jaime had changed her mind. Maybe...

"Sierra, what are you thinking?"

She turned away, embarrassed. "Nothing. I mean..." *Tell her already.* "I guess I was wondering why you won't let me in."

"Oh, is that all? Have I ever told you that you're cute when you blush?"

"Stop teasing me! Okay, you know my secret. Can I come in now?"

"Not yet."

"Why?"

"Because, silly. I can't let you in until I get a real morning kiss," Jaime said as if it were a well-known fact. "Ship rules."

"Really?" She narrowed her eyes and placed her hand in the center of Jaime's chest. She could feel Jaime's steady heartbeat beneath her T-shirt and used all her restraint not to brush her fingertips over the nipple hardening beneath the thin material. "And how many times since you've been on this ship have you invoked those rules?"

"Ooh, you're even cuter when you're jealous. But to answer your question, I lost count after the first—"

She pushed Jaime roughly into the room and slammed the door behind them. When Jaime lost her balance and fell backward onto the bed, she straddled Jaime's slim hips and pinned her hands to either side of her head. She leaned forward on all fours, letting her breasts sway inches from Jaime's lips.

"You listen to me, Jaime Rivers. The only *rules* you're allowed to follow from now on regarding anyone touching you are the ones I create. Understand?" She bent forward, nibbling her way down Jaime's neck and not caring if she sounded possessive. She finally had Jaime right where she wanted her, and nothing could stand in the way of that.

"Perfectly." Jaime groaned, turning her head so Sierra could feast. "I take it back. You're not just cute when you're jealous. You're sexy as hell."

"Glad you think so. I'm also not into sharing and you're changing the subject."

"Sorry. Where were we?" Jaime hissed when Sierra bit her neck.

"Remember now?" She soothed the bite with her tongue before tracing a path with it toward Jaime's ear. She traced each sensitive ridge as Jaime squirmed below her.

"Something about rules…please don't stop."

"Oh, I don't plan to stop. Listen closely. Rule one. From today on, no one kisses you but me."

She took Jaime's lower lip between her teeth and bit gently, tugging on Jaime's lip and eliciting a deep guttural groan. Slowly, she traced the rest of Jaime's lips, making sure not to leave any delicate skin unaccounted for.

"Sierra—"

"Shh. No talking until I'm done. Rule two. No one touches you but me."

She sat back on her heels and firmly rubbed her hands over Jaime's chest, pulling on Jaime's nipples through her T-shirt. Jaime bit her lip and grabbed for Sierra's hands, twining their fingers together and holding them tighter to her chest. Moisture pooled between her thighs, but she ignored her own pleasure, intent on keeping Jaime's attentions rather than gratifying herself. Cupping Jaime over her cotton boxers, she smiled when Jaime's eyes turned hazy and dark with need.

"Ah, baby. You can't do that. I'm so hard for you already. You don't know—"

"Shh, sweetheart. I'm not done." She found Jaime's clit underneath the soft material. Squeezing gently on either side, she forced Jaime's hips to push off the bed.

"God, yes. Harder, baby."

"Not until you agree to rule three. Jaime, are you listening?"

Jaime hissed as she pinched her clit. Not hard enough to make her come but just enough to keep her on the edge. "Jesus!"

"Listen to me, sweetheart. This is the most important rule."

"I'm...listening...ah..."

"No one makes love to you but me."

Jaime's head thrashed from side to side, as if trying to comprehend everything she was saying to her. "Need you...inside... so bad."

"I know, baby. I know. But I need you to tell me something first."

"Any...anything."

Jaime balancing on the edge of desire was a true sight to behold—head thrown back, body taut and tight, gripping the sheets as if anchoring herself through the storm raging within her body. Quickly relinquishing her possession on Jaime's clit, she released Jaime in more ways than one. Jaime cried out.

"Tell me, Jaime. Tell me you've thought about me over the last ten years. Tell me it wasn't just me that dreamed about being with you like this." She curled her body against Jaime's, tracing idle circles on her stomach on top of the thin T-shirt.

Sierra needed something, anything, that proved she wasn't the only one experiencing the deep connection she'd always felt between them. She had to hear from Jaime that she wasn't the only one that had suffered from their separation, that the spark that always made her insides tingle when Jaime was near affected Jaime with the same shocking intensity. That her touch made Jaime's blood run hot and that only her lips and the glide of her fingertips could quench that heat and make Jaime cry out for more.

Jaime had said she'd wanted to wait, but she felt the need to claim Jaime, her jealousy and uncertainty winning out over the promise to go slow. Hadn't ten years been a long-enough wait? Yeah, their relationship was in its early stages. And she would have never moved this fast with anyone else. But Jaime did crazy things to her, made her feel elated, irrational, and desired all with just a look. Now as Jaime pleaded for her to take whatever she wanted, she worried that maybe after Jaime came out of her sex-induced haze she'd regret not giving their relationship a little more time to mature. For all she knew, maybe Jaime wouldn't like this side of her. The jealous, possessive side that caused her to question Jaime's motives that morning before pushing Jaime back into her room to climb into bed with her. But as Jaime arched below her, bracing on the brink of orgasm, she had to know.

The breath flew from Jaime's chest as Sierra's hand traveled the length of her inner thigh and inched toward her stomach. As she moved closer to Jaime's belly button, she cried out again, but this time it wasn't a cry of passion. Before she knew what was happening, Jaime pushed her from her body and rolled onto her side into a fetal position. Sierra watched helplessly as Jaime threw her hands over her face and cried.

Oh no. Not again. "Hey." She rubbed Jaime's shoulder in an effort to calm her. "Baby, look at me."

Jaime refused to turn around, clutching her side as if protecting it from repetitive blows. She was shaking. "I...I can't."

"Honey, you're scaring me. You need to stop this and tell me what's going on."

"Sierra, you should go. Please."

"No. Not until we talk. I'm not going to allow you to shut me out this time. I know you have something to tell me. Whatever it is, I'm staying here until you do. No more secrets between us. I refuse to lose any more time with you."

"Oh, Christ. How did I ever live before you?" Jaime said, turning over to bury her face into Sierra's stomach.

She sifted Jaime's short hair between her fingers. "Let me be here for you. Let me in."

Several moments later, Jaime composed herself enough to recline against the headboard, motioning for Sierra to lie by her side. Jaime wiped at her tear-streaked face. "I'm sorry. Still think I'm a hero after that display?"

She stroked Jaime's abdomen in small circles, feeling Jaime relax under the gentle caress. "You will always be my hero. Even heroes cry, Jaime."

Jaime kissed her forehead, halting the caress. "If you want me to talk, you need to stop touching me like that."

"Like this?" she said, dipping her hand into Jaime's shorts.

Jaime's legs parted automatically, but after a few insistent caresses over her already throbbing clitoris she cried out weakly for Sierra to stop. Inhaling deeply, she visibly steadied herself. "Would you believe me if I told you I want to follow every one of those rules? But before I do, I have to tell you something important."

"Of course I believe you. You don't think I can see how you feel about me in your eyes? Or how you respond to me when we kiss? When we touch? I know we only really found each other last night, but it was like the last ten years never existed for me."

"For me too. But what would you say if I told you that what I have to tell you might change the way you feel about me?"

Sierra wanted to tell Jaime that no matter what she told her, her feelings would never change. She stopped herself from doing so, because something in Jaime's eyes told her that no matter what she promised, Jaime wouldn't believe her. Trust was still an issue between them, but she hoped to remedy that with time. "I'm listening."

Jaime's hands fidgeted nervously on her thighs and her lips trembled. "Do you remember how I used to love to surf?"

"How could I forget? I spent every waking moment with you at the beach. If you weren't in class, you were in the water doing crazy stunts on your board."

"And all this time I thought you hadn't been paying attention."

"Oh, no. I paid attention." She kissed one of Jaime's nipples hiding beneath her tee, feeling it pebble under the soft cotton. Jaime groaned. "Finish your story."

"I will if you stop that."

"Okay, stopped. Continue."

"Five years ago, I was practicing for the Half Moon Bay surfing championship. I was ranked number three in the country and had a pretty good shot at the title. During one of my practice sets, I was waiting for the perfect wave when I ran into something with my board. Or, rather, something ran into me."

"What was it?"

"Patience, love. I'm getting there. At first, I thought I'd hit a rock or maybe I'd imagined it. No one had ever hit anything that far out before. I spent the next few seconds scanning the water but didn't see anything. The second time it knocked me into the water and that's when everything went black. That's the last thing I remember."

"What are you saying?"

Jaime pushed off the bed and moved to stand directly in front of her. Without releasing her hold on Sierra's eyes, she yanked her T-shirt over her head and waited for Sierra's reaction. "I'm saying it wasn't a rock."

❖

Jaime stared at Sierra, cautiously gauging her reaction. She knew the horror all too well that Sierra was witnessing. She had to look at herself in the mirror daily. She'd memorized every inch of scar tissue from where her six-pack abs once were. Now, sections of mangled tissue and thick red teeth marks outlined where the shark had bitten into her flesh. Jagged scars ran in no apparent pattern over the left side of her abdomen and disappeared behind her back. Her breasts were still round and firm, thankfully left untouched. The other side of her body was perfect. The drastic difference between the two sides created a macabre fun-house effect.

Over time she'd learned to live with what she couldn't change, but what was scaring her now was that for the first time since she and Sierra had been reunited, she couldn't read anything in Sierra's expression. The questioning, guarded look was almost as if she'd disconnected herself from the horror she was witnessing. She'd figured Sierra probably wouldn't take the news well, but she hadn't expected silence. The longer Sierra stayed silent, the more the burning lump in her throat intensified.

Sierra's eyes misted and Jaime's insides plummeted. She wanted to cower in a corner, hide from Sierra and try to banish the look of torment on Sierra's face. She'd learned to live with rejection her whole life—her mom's leaving, her father's constant travels, her difficulty developing lasting friendships. But from Sierra it just plain hurt. She started to pull her shirt back over her head but was stopped short when Sierra grabbed the shirt. "Sierra, it's okay. You don't have to—"

"Shush," Sierra said tenderly, moving to a kneeling position in front of her. Sierra ran her hand over the uneven tissue as she remained motionless, scarcely breathing. Goose bumps formed on her skin and Sierra raised her head to meet her gaze. "Does it hurt?" Sierra asked, kissing each section of uneven tissue.

"Sometimes." Her voice grew deeper. "But not when you do that."

"Then I need to do it more often." Sierra framed her waist with her hands and rubbed her cheek along the rough scars.

"I can't believe you still want to touch me like this after finding out." She moaned, running her fingers through Sierra's hair as her tongue traced the length of another scar.

"Why, because of a few scars?" Sierra linked her fingers through hers. "Do you really think I'm that shallow?"

"No, of course not. But look at me." She opened her arms to give Sierra a full view. "You have to admit, this is not very attractive."

"Jaime, Jaime, Jaime," Sierra said, "What am I going to do with you?"

"I can think of a number of things," she whispered as Sierra stood and wrapped her arms around her neck.

"And I can add to that list." Sierra leaned in for a quick kiss, grabbed her face, and stared deeply into her eyes. "But first I want you to listen to me closely. I don't care how many scars you have, you will always be beautiful to me. All I care about is that we're always honest with each other. As long as we have trust, we can work anything out."

Her smile faltered and she tried to look away, but Sierra refused to release her.

"No you don't. Look at me. I'm right here. So is this your big secret?"

"Yes." *No. One of them, anyway.* Christ, Sierra was talking about honesty and she still hadn't told her about her past addiction issues. Maybe she could look past the scars. But would adding addiction to the mixture be too much to ask Sierra to handle? The moment felt too fragile to push it any further, even though she knew she needed to.

"Then you have nothing to worry about." Sierra leaned forward and took her ear in between her teeth, then bit lightly.

She shivered. "I want to believe that."

"You'd better. We'll talk more about this later, but right now we have to stop. And before you get all concerned on me...no, it's not what I want, but the gift I had planned to give you this morning can't wait."

"You mean this wasn't it?" She reached between Sierra's legs and squeezed gently.

"Oh, God!" Sierra thrust her hips forward into her hand. "Unfortunately not. It's a paid excursion to climb the waterfall at Dunn's River Falls. Two of the guests came down with food poisoning last night, so I managed to snag the last two tickets. The boat that takes us to the falls leaves in," she looked at the clock, "twenty minutes. Believe me. If I knew we were going to end up in here together like this, I wouldn't have…Oh!" She jerked in surprise when Jaime squeezed, again.

"What was that?" Jaime finally released Sierra and stepped out of reach, grinning at the look of frustration on Sierra's face.

"Hey, what gives—"

"Thanks for the gift. Hopefully that will keep you thinking about me while we climb the waterfall," she said, and dodged a pillow aimed at her head before ducking into the bathroom to change.

"Tease!"

She braced her arms against the bathroom sink, her skin still tingling from Sierra's touch. She still needed to say so much to Sierra, but for now she welcomed the opportunity to get to know her. Maybe by the time the cruise was over, she would know if Sierra could handle the truth. She couldn't fathom what she would do if she lost her again.

CHAPTER TWELVE

Jaime looked up at the cascading wall of water tumbling down the mammoth rock formations of Dunn's River Falls. On the half-hour trip by catamaran to the falls, Sierra gave her some history about the falls in Ocho Rios. She listened to the tour guide as well, as he explained that geologists call the falls a living phenomenon because they are continuously rebuilt from deposits of calcium carbonate and sodium from the river water. They were also one of very few falls that emptied directly into the ocean. Wishing she had a pen and paper handy, she suddenly imagined Flynn climbing the falls effortlessly to rescue some damsel in distress hanging from one of the protruding rocks. Maybe she'd write that story line into her next book, if she could ever get the damn thing written.

"Jaime?" Sierra said, reaching for her hand.

"Yeah, sorry. You were saying?"

"Wasn't saying anything. They're getting ready for us to climb the first part. Having a Flynn moment?"

"How'd you guess that?" she asked curiously.

"Easy. You get this gleam in your eye when you're thinking about something…let's just say adventurous."

"Is that so," she said, pulling Sierra closer. She bit Sierra's neck playfully and received a playful shove.

"Stop that. You're going to get me all hot and bothered again. I can't climb and be swollen at the same time."

"Come here." She pulled Sierra back to her and kissed her sweetly. "I kinda like you hard for me."

"That's it." Sierra stepped into her, a dangerous glint in her eyes, and lowered her voice so that only Jaime could hear her. "I'm hard all the time where you're concerned." Sierra rimmed her ear with her tongue. "But now, so are you."

"No fair."

"I'll give you a chance to get even later."

Christ, how did Sierra always know how to rock her world? She was hard, but the thought of Sierra suffering too made the pain pounding in her groin bearable. She tried to focus on the guide's instructions regarding the human chain formed to climb the falls. She couldn't help stressing over the fact that everyone but her had stripped down to a bathing suit. Still in her board shorts and T-shirt, she hadn't thought of the ninety plus heat that was common in a tropical paradise. She wished she didn't have to wear a shirt, but she didn't want to scare the tourists or embarrass herself. Or worse, Sierra.When she heard the tour guides tell them to deposit their valuables and clothes on the picnic table designated for their group, her anxiety flared into panic.

"I know what you're thinking." Sierra wrapped her arms around her waist from behind and kissed her shoulder. "You're beautiful, baby."

"I'm glad you think so. But really, Sierra…come on. These people are going to think I'm some kind of freak."

"If anyone even looks at you cross-eyed, they'll have to answer to me. Now take your shirt off, handsome. We need to hurry."

Reluctantly, Jaime did as instructed, glancing around nervously even though the one-piece suit she was wearing under her board shorts hid a majority of her scars. Listening intently as the guide explained how they would be part of the next human chain that would be climbing up the first half of the six-hundred-foot section of waterfalls, she wondered if Sierra was nervous about the climb.

"Ready?" Sierra stood before her in what little there was of the navy-blue bikini that left little to the imagination. The smile on Sierra's face indicated she'd achieved her desired effect.

"Sierra, when did you—"

"Change?"

"Yeah." She realized she probably sounded like a blundering idiot, but this wasn't the one-piece Sierra had worn to her room that morning.

Sierra laughed. "When you went into the bathroom. I wanted to surprise you."

"You did," she murmured. Her voice was lower than normal, even to her own ears, but she couldn't control it or her body's reaction to the beautiful sight before her.

"Hold that thought that made your pupils dilate to the size of marbles," Sierra whispered before giving her a quick kiss.

"You're killing me."

"Good. Let's go."

The first part of the climb was the steepest and the slickest. As the climb progressed, it became apparent why a human chain was used to advance up the falls. Every so often, someone would lose traction and slip. If the person next to them wasn't paying attention, they were likely to fall with them, usually ending up in one of the many small pools, if they were lucky. Everyone seemed to be laughing and having a good time, but all she could concentrate on was Sierra's barely covered body poised on the rocks below her, waiting for her to give her a hand up to the next section of falls. Luckily for her, it also offered a clear view of the same perky breasts that had held her attention the night before.

Halfway up the falls, the group huddled around a large pool where climbers were allowed to jump in while one of the Jamaican tour guides took pictures of them making their most spectacular leaps. When it came time for Jaime and Sierra to jump, Sierra didn't wait for the guide to say "jump," pushing her playfully backward into the pool. Her natural reaction was to reach for the closest object, which happened to be Sierra. Her awkward flailing caused her to grab Sierra's bathing-suit top instead, pulling Sierra into the water and unintentionally yanking the top off in the process.

Sierra fell into the water with a scream as Jaime surfaced seconds later, dangling the bikini top between her fingers like a trophy. The cheers and whistles that followed only egged her on to twirl it higher above her head.

"Give me that," Sierra said, emerging from below the surface with one arm covering her breasts and the other reaching for the top. Sierra eventually yanked her under the water, wrestling the top away from her without much of a fight. She managed to put her top back on without much difficulty before returning to the surface. "I can't believe you did that!"

"That's what you get," she said with a laugh before climbing out of the pool and assisting Sierra.

"Why, what did I do?"

She pulled Sierra close and whispered, "You've been teasing me all day. First with your surprise visit this morning and now prancing around barely wearing anything. Tell me you don't know the effect all that's having on me."

"Oh, I know," Sierra said running her nails up Jaime's back. "But because of that stunt, I've only just begun."

She didn't think she'd ever survive the rest of the day as Sierra sauntered off swinging her curvy hips, towel in hand. Luckily for her heart rate and her sanity, the rest of the climb was uneventful. After finally reaching the top, they decided to break away from the group to go for a swim underneath one of the many private waterfalls. They shared a slow kiss as the water danced all around them, but after two hours of climbing and the boat ride on the way to the falls, they were both ready for a little relaxation.

Sierra found a flat rock to stretch out on while Jaime dried off with a towel supplied by the ship. Sierra had to know that she was watching her, and when Sierra ran her hand down her stomach and let out a small groan, Jaime's mouth went dry.

"Do you enjoy taunting me," she asked darkly as she stalled the motion of the towel against her damp hair.

"Yes, but I'm enjoying the way you're looking at me more."

"Tell me. How am I looking at you?"

"Dangerously. I can almost taste the way you want me. Can see it in your eyes. They get all dark and stormy. When you look at me, you seem to be caressing me. Your body vibrates with tension, like a tightrope about to snap."

With two long strides she closed the gap between them. Bending forward, she took Sierra's lips firmly, possessively. When she leaned back, her only wish was that they were somewhere more private. Hovering above Sierra, she didn't know whether she should laugh or cry. The last four days had been surreal, but what would happen when the magical week ended?

They hadn't talked about the future. She hadn't even asked Sierra basic questions like where she lived. She'd been so engrossed in just being with her that she didn't want to contemplate anything past the week. Too many scary questions popped into her head as she looked down at the person who had always kept her world spinning out of control. What would happen once she told Sierra about her past? Would Sierra be able to handle it or would she want to return back to a life without Jaime in it? That morning Sierra said all she'd ever wanted was to be together, but would she think the same thing once Jaime came clean?

"Hey." Sierra touched her face tenderly. "Why so sad all of a sudden?"

Damn, Sierra had caught her wallowing again. Time to get her head in the game. She had to focus on the moment, more so if there was a possibility there wouldn't be many more of them. "Not sad. I guess we can't get away from some things no matter how hard we try."

"Wanna talk about it?"

She sat next to Sierra, her stomach tightening as Sierra made small circles against the tense muscles with her fingertips. "Eventually. But not here."

"Honey, whatever it is we'll figure it out together. There are things I need to tell you too. Let's make a deal. We enjoy the rest of our day together, and then after dinner you can treat me to an ice cream and we'll talk. What do you say?"

Her whole body relaxed. "Deal. Speaking of food, I heard someone say there's a cafeteria that serves spicy jerk chicken up here. My treat if you're interested?"

"Interested? Food is food. Lead the way."

She gathered up their things and followed Sierra to the food hut. Her confession would have to wait another few hours.

❖

Jaime returned from her afternoon out with Sierra to find Darlene sitting on one of the beds in their room, looking out of sorts. She had intended to ask Darlene all about the Jamaican Canopy tour that included zip-lining through Cranbrook Flower Forest. From the series of worry lines creasing Darlene's forehead, that would have to wait.

"Everything okay?" she asked.

"No. It's Rebecca."

Rebecca? What does she have to do with anything? "Okay, back up."

"She's here, Jaime."

"Here?" she asked in surprise. "You mean here as in Jamaica, or here as in on this ship?"

"I mean on this ship."

By the way Darlene fidgeted on the bed there was obviously more to the story. "I don't mean to be dense, but so? She has a right to vacation just like everyone else."

"If that was all she was doing I wouldn't be worried. She's drinking again, Jaime."

"Shit! Do you know where she is now?" Jaime rummaged through the piles of clothes in her closet, pulling out a pair of wrinkled jeans and a BillABong T-shirt.

"I have no idea, but she needed assistance to get back onto the boat. I tried to help but she told me to back off."

"Don't take it personally, Darlene. You know the situation. I'll take care of it."

Since her accident, being Rebecca Ripley's AA sponsor was the only meaningful thing Jaime had done except for writing. If she had learned anything from being in recovery it was that being someone's sponsor was a great responsibility. To this day, she still kept in touch with her sponsor when she needed someone to talk to, someone to sit and listen. She had introduced Rebecca to Darlene as a way for Rebecca to meet people outside her usual drinking buddies, and the three of them had hung out together several times, but lately she had been too wrapped up in her own issues to call and check on Rebecca. Clearly that had been a mistake. She grabbed her sunglasses and placed her ship's card in her pocket. "I'm going to go look for her. If Sierra comes by, tell her I went for a walk."

"Why? Can't I just say—"

"No! You can't. Got me?"

"Jesus, Jaime! You haven't told her yet?"

Jaime threw her hands over her ears and started chanting "la la la" not in the mood for one of Darlene's patronizing speeches. Like she didn't know the score. Of course, Darlene's intentions stemmed from being worried about her but her anger with both situations bubbled to the surface. She was tired of hiding the truth from Sierra, but she didn't need her best friend rubbing her nose in the dirt to prove her point. "Enough. I plan to explain everything tonight. Let me deal with this problem first."

"What are you going to do?"

"Find her," she said. "What else."

"But how do you know where to look?"

"Because she'll be in the same spot I would be if I were in her place."

CHAPTER THIRTEEN

Jaime walked out of the Tahitian-themed bar trying to figure out if there was any place on the ship she hadn't checked for Rebecca. Normally when she walked into a lounge or past a bar, she had to fight her own demons, the ones that urged her to sink back into the familiar. *Just one taste,* they always whispered. But today those impulses were surprisingly absent. Maybe it was because she was more concerned about Rebecca than her own well-being.

One of the rules of recovery was that a person needed to face her issues on her own, to want to get better, not desire what others wanted for her. Jaime had wanted to recover enough to kick the addiction, and with Sierra currently back in her life she wanted to even more. Regardless, every time she entered a bar, she couldn't help but experience the same hopelessness she felt during those first few days of not drinking. Acrid memories of the walls closing in all around her, suffocating her to the point that she either needed to break away and make it to the surface for air or drown herself in the familiar clung to her skin like smoke. She tried to shake the sensation off as she traipsed from bar to bar.

She'd never taken drugs to cope in social situations. Instead, she suffered quietly in her own private hell, away from prying eyes, avoiding social situations altogether. She didn't want others witnessing her pain, her failures. Every time she saw a lost soul drowning in a drink, she saw a mirror of the person she used to be. Drugs, alcohol, it was all the same—people engulfed in sorrow and selling their souls to hide from whatever ailed them.

She was about to call it quits, fatigue and frustration taking her to a place she didn't want to be, when she spotted Rebecca staggering out of a nearby bathroom. She climbed awkwardly onto a nearby bar stool, using a straw to twirl the light-brown concoction in front of her.

"Rebecca?" Jaime said quietly, trying not to startle her. A surprised drunk could be an unpredictable drunk.

Rebecca turned in her direction and raised her glass in salute. "I wondered how long it would take for Darlene to rat me out." Rebecca downed the liquid with one gulp. "Ah. Long time no see, Jaime."

"Sorry, it's been a while. How are you?"

"Cut the shit. We obviously know how I am."

Being Rebecca's sponsor had taught Jaime that everyone had a different way of dealing with their pain, but she didn't know how to get Rebecca out of the bar in her fragile state. "Something I can do?"

"Yeah. Go away." Rebecca motioned to the bartender for a refill as Jaime climbed onto the stool next to her. "I'm not in the mood for a pep talk tonight."

The bartender turned a questioning glance toward Jaime, who motioned for a cup of coffee instead. When the steaming mug arrived, she pushed it in front of Rebecca. "Here, why don't you drink this?"

"If I wanted coffee, I'd have asked for fucking coffee." Rebecca pushed the cup aside, spilling its contents all over the bar. "I said, go the hell away and leave me alone."

I wish it were that easy. "I'm sorry. I can't do that."

"Sure you can. Jack and Coke," she yelled to the bartender, but he pretended not to hear her.

Jaime was at a crossroads. There wasn't much she could do, short of dragging Rebecca out of the bar. That would stop her from drinking, but only momentarily, and there was no point if she didn't want to sober up. She'd learned firsthand that people recovering from an addiction had to admit they had a problem and acknowledge that they were powerless over a drug. They also had to appreciate that their life was manageable without a mind-altering substance. If

Rebecca had lost her way, all Jaime could do was offer assistance in guiding her back to the right path.

"Wanna talk about it?" she asked.

"Nothing to say."

"Rebecca," she said gently. "You're drowning yourself in alcohol. There's plenty to say."

Rebecca turned tear-stained cheeks to her. "Nobody wants me."

She had no idea what Rebecca was talking about, but at least she was talking. "Tell me. Talking helps. Believe me, I know."

"I don't want your fucking help!" Rebecca pointed to the tumbler in an effort to get the bartender's attention again, but this time Jaime pushed it out of her reach. "Damn it, Jaime. Back off. I need that."

"No, you don't. You need to sleep, but first, I need to know what's going on."

"Fine. You wanna know what's wrong? I'll tell you what's fucking wrong." Rebecca was nearly screaming now, but thankfully it was still too early for the happy-hour crowd. "I came out of that damn program feeling like my old self. I tried going back to a normal life—a normal routine. And you know what happened? My husband was gone. My friends didn't like me anymore because I didn't drink and I wasn't any fun. Hell, I haven't been able to find work in over a year. I look in the mirror and I don't even like myself. If I don't like the new me, how is anyone else going to like me? I'm a failure. A complete and total failure."

She stared at Rebecca, remembering a similar conversation with Darlene a few weeks ago. She wanted to tell Rebecca that she was a beautiful person who deserved more credit than she was giving herself, that she'd always be there for her no matter what, but she knew any words she uttered couldn't penetrate the alcohol-induced fog that currently overshadowed Rebecca's reality. Suddenly, sitting there watching Rebecca fall apart, she glimpsed how she must have appeared to Darlene when she was at her worst. She felt sorry and thankful for Darlene but also glad Sierra had never had to witness this side of her.

"What? No words of wisdom, oh great sponsor?"

That did it. She'd had enough of the poor-me routine. Yanking Rebecca off her stool, she decided that Rebecca didn't need wisdom; she needed a meeting. For once she was happy she hadn't tuned Darlene and her agonizing list of ship's activities out completely.

"Hey, let go!"

"Not a chance."

Rebecca stumbled out of the bar after her, Jaime doing her best to keep her upright. "Jesus, will you slow down," Rebecca said loudly, drawing a few curious stares. "Fuck, I'm going to vomit. Stop!"

"Not until we get where we're going. I think it's time for you to meet Lois R and her friends."

"Who?"

"You'll see."

❖

Sierra stared absently at her appetizer fork, wondering why Jaime hadn't arrived for dinner yet. She hated feeling needy and insecure. She'd never been clingy before and hated when someone constantly wanted to hold hands or touch in general. Even something as simple as a hand on her knee during dinner would typically irritate the hell out of her, except when Jaime did it. All day Jaime had stayed by her side. They'd held hands after climbing the waterfall, sat close enough for their legs to touch at lunch, and Jaime had caressed her thigh or rested her hand possessively on her back throughout the day. Not only did Sierra like the contact, she craved it. Its absence made her extra aware that Jaime wasn't beside her.

Breathing deeply, she fought the urge to flee. Years of therapy had helped her understand that she coped by running from things she was scared of. Of course, fleeing when things became difficult wasn't healthy, but at least once she recognized the behavior she could deal with it. She'd been a stronger, bolder person ever since.

So why did those insecurities resurface every time Jaime was absent? These last few days had been some of the happiest of her life, apart from the years she and Jaime had spent together in high school. She loved everything about Jaime, from the way she walked confidently with her shoulders back and head high to the way she'd moaned when Sierra had touched her for the first time. She'd never tire of Jaime's deep voice that only grew huskier when Jaime would whisper her name.

But every time she looked into Jaime's eyes, she sensed her reticence, her caution. Something besides the shark attack had happened in Jaime's past that was causing her tremendous pain, and she wanted desperately to know what that something was. Jaime had promised her they'd talk tonight—was that why she was avoiding dinner? Whatever the reason, she couldn't sit at the table any longer. Politely excusing herself, she opted for a walk, hoping to burn off the flare of anxiety burning a hole in her gut.

Heading toward the bow of the ship, she leaned against the railing and closed her eyes, recalling passion-filled kisses that had turned her world upside down. A tinge of salt tickled her tongue and it was impossible to determine whether it had come from her tears or the fine mist that blew in from the sea. She tried not to cry, but the emotional tidal wave she'd been riding since running into Jaime had left her more vulnerable than she could remember since high school.

Something had to have happened for Jaime to have stood her up for dinner. Darlene didn't show either, so maybe they'd decided to skip dinner and hang out, given that Sierra had been monopolizing most of Jaime's time since the cruise began. After all, Darlene was Jaime's friend too. Didn't she deserve some of Jaime's time? The answer was simple but didn't make the familiar pangs of jealousy that surfaced hurt any less.

She didn't have to dig deep to figure out why their friendship bothered her so much. She still longed to be Jaime's best friend. She should have been the one sitting by Jaime's side after one of nature's fiercest creatures attacked her while she was doing a sport she loved. She should have been the one whispering words of encouragement to Jaime while she healed, the one to kiss the tears of pain away that she knew Jaime must have shed. Thinking about Jaime suffering in any way brought on a fresh batch of tears. She leaned forward on the ship's railing and peered over the side, watching her teardrops fall and become one with the waves. The ocean seemed as vacant as her heart, but as the waves crashed against the ship, she was reminded that even though life seemed empty at times, powerful forces still existed. She felt someone behind her and relief flooded her when Jaime spoke.

"Please don't jump," Jaime said softly. "If I have to go in after you, I may drown us both."

She turned and smiled faintly. "Like I'd jump off a perfectly good boat."

"Hey, what's with the tears?" Jaime moved closer, her voice full of curiosity and worry.

She flung her body into Jaime's waiting arms, burying her face in Jaime's shoulder. "It's—"

"Shh, calm down. I'm here. I'm here, baby." Jaime rubbed her back in soothing circles as she struggled for breath. "If it's about dinner, I'm sorry. I fell asleep and lost track of time. Forgive me?"

She kept her arms firmly around Jaime's waist, refusing to move from the circle of her arms. She didn't want to tell Jaime that when she didn't show up for dinner she'd panicked, that she'd been worried from the moment they'd reunited that something would take Jaime away from her again. That idea had frightened her so much she found it impossible to sit through dinner. She'd wanted to prove that she was stronger, that she had the ability to handle almost any situation. But just the thought of losing Jaime was so overpowering, she crumbled from the pressure.

Of course she was being irrational. Jaime was here, wrapped in her arms. How could she explain her momentary lapse of sanity? Jaime would think she was being ridiculous or even too clingy after only a few days.

"Sierra, please. Talk to me."

She pulled back a little, wiping her eyes with her palms. "Promise you won't think I'm nuts?"

"Swear."

"You didn't come to dinner and I got...scared."

"What scared you?"

She buried her face in Jaime's chest, suddenly feeling remarkably foolish. "You leaving me. Silly, huh?"

"Oh, baby, I just found you," Jaime said, getting Sierra to look at her. "How could you think I'd leave you?"

Jaime's expression was so serious and so tender it took her breath away. "I told you I was being silly."

"No, not silly. I'm so sorry for being late. Honest."

"You don't have to be sorry. I shouldn't have assumed—"

Jaime interrupted her rambling with a kiss, pulling her tight to her body. The heat between them caused her to succumb instantly, her body melting into the inferno that was Jaime's mouth.

"I don't think I'll ever get enough of you," Jaime said, holding her close.

"I feel the same."

"Look, we should talk," she finally said, when she got enough oxygen back into her lungs.

"Whatever you want. But food first," Jaime said, her breathing shallow and uneven. "We need a quiet place and something to eat, since it seems we both skipped dinner."

"Sounds good to me but where? We're on a ship with five hundred of our classmates. We haven't had quiet since we stepped on this damn boat."

Jaime laughed. "I couldn't agree more. Since it's getting late, the bars will be busy. We're going someplace none of them will be."

"And that is…"

"The ice-cream parlor, of course," Jaime said, wiggling her eyebrows playfully.

"Rocky Road?"

"Yep."

"Ooh. You definitely know the way to a girl's heart."

Jaime kissed her knuckles. "Only this girl's."

"You just remember that, Rivers."

"Don't worry." Jaime gave her a long, lingering kiss. "I will."

CHAPTER FOURTEEN

Sierra gathered up her sundae and followed Jaime to the back of the empty ice-cream parlor. Moaning in delight during her second spoonful of pure chocolate bliss, she took her time enjoying the rich combination of chocolate, sweet marshmallows, and crunchy nuts. Thankfully, indulging in one of her favorite obsessions was a great way to compensate for sexual frustration. Not helping matters was Jaime's tongue snaking out from between her lips to take long, slow swipes at her spoon.

"Like that, do ya?" She fought back a groan when Jaime wiped the edge of her lips clean with her tongue.

"Yep. Nothing beats a good banana split." Jaime rested the curved part of the spoon against her tongue, sucking slowly on the last remnants of her ice cream. Her eyes glinted dangerously.

"You know, two can play that game."

"Who's playing? Besides, I remember someone being quite the tease earlier."

"I guess you're right. Since you seem to be enjoying yours so much better than mine, let's see if yours tastes better." Holding Jaime's challenging stare, she used her spoon to swipe a generous amount of Jaime's whipped cream, then held the spoon close to her mouth and licked slowly, not willing to waste any of the sweet cream. Losing herself in Jaime's hot gaze, she envisioned having Jaime sprawled naked on one of the ship's deck chairs. She'd take her time and use her tongue to explore every delicious inch of her, teasing Jaime with a mixture of teeth and lips. Jaime would arch below her and cry out—

"Sierra, what are you thinking?"

She put her spoon down, propping her elbows on the table. "If you couldn't tell by my display, I'm going to have to try harder."

"Tell me." Jaime's voice was rough. "I want to hear it."

She motioned Jaime closer with her finger and whispered, "Let me put it this way. I wish you were this spoon."

"Jesus! You're going to give me a heart attack."

"Funny. That wasn't the part of the body I was trying to excite. By the way, nice shade. You're pretty adorable when you blush."

"Cut it out!"

She laughed. "Okay, fine. Seriously, though. Can I ask you a question?"

"Anything."

"Did I at least make you wet?"

Jaime groaned as if she were in pain, but her heated gaze and flushed skin said that the kind of pain she was suffering from wasn't allowing her to remain comfortably seated. She closed her eyes. "You promised."

"You're right. I did. And I don't intend to break that promise. But once we've said our piece, all bets are off."

"I can see that playing with you is going to be like playing with fire."

"Absolutely, but I promise I won't burn you." She linked her fingers with Jaime's.

"I trust you. But I may need a cold shower before we talk about anything serious."

"No you don't. I kind of like you all hot and bothered. Turns me on."

"Damn it, Sierra. Stop!"

"Fine, fine." She'd made her point. No need to reduce Jaime to a smoldering pile of ashes, at least not here and not yet. "We came to talk. You ask the first question."

Jaime sat quietly for a moment and Sierra could almost see the wheels spinning wildly in her head. If Jaime thought any harder, she was certain she'd see steam coming out Jaime's ears.

"Okay. Let's start with the story of when you first knew you were gay."

She wasn't surprised by the question and wondered why it had taken Jaime so long to ask. Part of her wanted to say high school, but she didn't think Jaime would believe her, especially since she'd walked out on her. Not willing to chance bringing up old hurts, she chose safer ground. "I just knew."

"Have you been with a lot of women?"

"Depends on your definition of 'been with.'"

"Well…you know."

"Let's just say I've dated many women," she said, so Jaime would stop squirming. "But I've only kissed two. That includes you."

"Wait, what?" Jaime's eyes were wide. "That can't be. How could you know—"

"No!" she said softly, defiantly. The cloud of doubt was back but this time for an entirely different reason. "Please, don't doubt this. What I feel for you is real. I know what I'm doing. This isn't a test run for me."

"But how do you know? I've known since I was fourteen. I don't think I could handle it if you decided to change your mind."

"I won't change my mind. Please, Jaime. You have to trust me."

"I want to. Believe me," Jaime said, the agony in her words matching the pain etched on her face. "But before we go any further, you need to know something about me."

"Tell me." She stroked Jaime's trembling jaw. She hated to see her in pain.

"I will but not here," Jaime said, pulling her to her feet. "Let's go back to your room. What I have to say, I need to say in private."

❖

Jaime clung to Sierra's hand, waiting impatiently for her to open up the door to her stateroom. By the time she was ushered in, she felt like she might vomit. The room began to spin and it took all her energy not to hyperventilate. Thankfully she sank into a chair before her legs gave way. Anywhere was better than sitting next to Sierra on the bed because she couldn't confess a thing with Sierra touching her.

"Jaime, you look like you're about to keel over. Believe me, I'm a big girl and can handle whatever you throw at me."

Let's hope so. She rubbed her hands over her legs—anything to keep them from shaking. "It's not that I don't believe you, but what I'm about to say may be difficult for you to hear. You see… tonight…when I missed dinner…I was with…" Shit! It'd been so much easier when she'd rehearsed it.

"Jaime, trust me, whatever it is, it can't be that bad."

Sierra's warm hands enfolded hers, and the second she looked into Sierra's eyes all her defenses crumbled. "Of course I trust you. Don't you get what I'm trying to say? It's me you shouldn't trust."

Sierra sat back and released her hands. "Go on."

"Earlier, when I missed dinner, I was helping out a friend. When I returned to my room I was exhausted and fell asleep. That's why I was late."

"A friend? You mean Darlene?"

"No. This was someone else."

She judged Sierra's reaction carefully as different emotions swept over her face. Curiosity. Anger. But the last one, hurt, punched through Jaime's awareness, knocking the breath from her chest.

"Is this *friend* someone special?" Sierra asked, her voice breaking.

The pain in Sierra's voice pierced her heart like molten steel through her flesh. She reacted instantly, kneeling between Sierra's legs, careful not to touch her. "Yes, she is. But not in the way you're probably thinking."

"Really?" Sierra choked. "And just what am I thinking?"

"That it's some type of romantic involvement. It's not, Sierra. Swear. Her name is Rebecca. And I'm her…sponsor."

"I'm sorry," Sierra asked, hurt morphing into confusion. "I'm not quite following."

She inhaled deeply. "This is what I've been trying to tell you. I'm a recovering addict."

Sierra sat motionless, looking shocked, and then, as if someone had shut down a computer screen, her expression went blank. She didn't respond. Hell, she didn't even blink.

"Sierra, please," she said, placing a hand on Sierra's knee and wincing when she pulled her leg away. "Say something."

Sierra lost all awareness of time as the room receded from view. She no longer saw Jaime kneeling in front of her. Instead she was sitting on an emergency-room table the night she'd left Eric. A nurse was asking her all sorts of questions, but like then, she couldn't find the words. Her eye was swollen shut, her lip split, her ego bruised. This couldn't be happening. How could she have been so stupid to have been deceived again?

"Sierra, please. The silence is killing me."

"I think it's time I told you about Eric," she said.

"Okay."

She moved to the other side of the room, incapable of being near Jaime now. She didn't want anything to distract her from what she was about to tell her. "I met Eric while I was in college. He was good-looking, smart. We married after he graduated. It was okay at first. I always knew something was missing, but I couldn't put my finger on exactly what that was. He used to drink occasionally. One glass of wine a night turned into two. One party flowed into the next. Pretty soon, he drank from the time he woke up in the morning until he passed out at night. By that time, I wanted a divorce. I realized I didn't love him and, really, I never had. I even caught him with another woman in our bed. That was the night I told him to leave. God, I was so happy I caught him cheating on me because it gave me an excuse to get him out of my life."

Jaime listened intently, never moving, hardly breathing. "Sierra, I can only imagine—"

"Let me finish." She impatiently waved her hand. "After the first few lies I caught him in, I couldn't trust him. I never believed what he told me. I caught him lying so many times I finally gave up on him ever telling me the truth. The night I asked him to leave, he swore that the woman in our bed was just a friend, told me it would never happen again. I told him to go to hell. He hit me." Her voice broke.

"Oh, God." Jaime moved across the room and, taking Sierra into her arms, kissed her on the top of her head but stepped back when Sierra tensed. "I'm so sorry he hurt you."

"I believe you. But I don't think you understand that since then, I've developed trust issues. I've always trusted you. You never gave me a reason to doubt you, until now. I can't trust an addict, Jaime. I've been there, done that."

"Sierra," she said, her voice hoarse. "I'm just asking for a chance. I can make this right. I know I can. Swear."

"No!" Sierra pushed past her. "You don't get to say that to me. Not after everything I thought we meant to each other. How can you expect me to trust you when you've been keeping this secret from me for days? I swore after Eric that I would never be involved with someone with addiction issues again, that I'd never go through the pain and suffering of watching them deteriorate day after day or worry about them slipping up when they were the least bit stressed. You allowed me to believe in you, to believe I'd get my chance at a normal relationship. You showed me your scars, told me about the attack. But you left out the part about being an addict when you could have told me. Why you? Why you!"

Sierra collapsed into Jaime's arms at the same moment Jaime's world tumbled down around her. This was what she'd feared since running into Sierra—that Sierra wouldn't be able to deal with her past and would leave her. As old abandonment issues surfaced, she thought about the pain of her mother walking out and the many lonely nights of waiting by the window for her father to return. She'd never be able to survive the loss of Sierra again, and she couldn't even pretend she could.

She had to make Sierra understand just how much she cared about her. To tell her every day if she had to, so that she could earn back that trust. "Please." She knew she was begging and didn't care. She held Sierra's head between her hands, trying to get her to look at her. "I can't make you believe anything I'm saying, but I'm willing to prove to you every day with every kiss and touch that you can trust me. All I'm asking for is that chance."

Sierra moved into her arms and placed her head on Jaime's shoulder. "I want to believe in you. I do. But I don't know if I can do it. I'm scared."

"You're not the only one," she whispered. "I wanted this so much with you that I was scared to tell you. So much that you had to know everything about me before we went any further. Nothing has to happen tonight, but please understand that you're all that matters to me."

She pulled Sierra into a firm hug, the gentle resistance breaking her heart. After a moment Sierra relaxed and Jaime closed her eyes, grateful for the momentary reprieve.

"So, where do we go from here,"she asked tentatively, not remembering a time in her life when an answer from someone had ever meant so much. "I want you, Sierra. You know my demons now. There's nothing left you don't know about me. Please, don't send me away."

Sierra pulled back and looked at her for a long moment, searching her eyes before she spoke. "I won't send you away and I don't want to wait any longer. Can we agree, just for tonight, to keep the past in the past and just enjoy being with each other?"

She kissed Sierra fiercely, hoping that was answer enough, at least for one night.

CHAPTER FIFTEEN

"Don't look so nervous," Sierra said, pushing Jaime up against the stateroom door. She ran her hands up both sides of Jaime's long torso. Jaime hissed.

"Easy for you to say. Can you blame me for wanting this to be special?"

"Oh, it will be." She combed her hands through Jaime's short blond hair, pressing her body along the length of her. The kiss wasn't gentle nor was it meant to be. Slipping one of her legs between Jaime's longer ones, she bit along Jaime's jaw as Jaime clutched the doorframe for support.

"Sierra, you're going to destroy me." Jaime groaned when she gently bit her earlobe.

"That's the plan." She placed her hand between Jaime's legs, squeezing hard enough to make Jaime's hips jerk forward. "I can feel your heat. You're ready for me, aren't you?"

Jaime released the doorframe, placing her hands on Sierra's hips. The mask of insecurity had vanished, and in its place was a look of longing and desire that made her skin tingle and her blood boil.

"Always," Jaime said, crushing Sierra's smaller body to hers.

Jaime reached around to the back of her dress and slowly lowered the zipper. Kissing each expanse of bare skin that was revealed, Jaime descended until she was kneeling in front of her with the dress pooled at her feet. "My God, look at you."

She placed her hand on Jaime's jaw, holding her steady gaze. "I love the way you look at me." *But can I trust this is how you truly feel or is this your need talking?* "Take me, please. I can't wait much longer."

Jaime slid her hands up the inside of Sierra's thighs, hooking her fingers through the silky red thong, pulling the material tight to Sierra's body. She tilted her hips forward as Jaime used her tongue to toy with the swollen prominence of her need bulging beneath the soft material.

"Oh, please." She groaned.

Jaime removed the thong altogether, throwing it somewhere behind her. She stood, picking Sierra up by her hips so she could hook her legs around Jaime's middle.

"What are you doing?"

"You'll see," Jaime said, as she yanked the blanket off the bed with one hand while holding her up with the other.

Jaime padded the large windowsill behind them, placing her comfortably inside. She reclined against some pillows, leaving her legs open and her body exposed. Jaime knelt reverently before her, framing her sex with her fingers.

"This is very creative of you," she said as Jaime trailed a few kisses inside her thighs and a moan escaped her lips.

"You know us authors. Always striving to be different." Jaime lowered her mouth, taking Sierra's quivering flesh between her lips. She slowly took her time to trace each ridge and tender fold, as if savoring the taste of a fine wine. Sierra's hips surged against her face, the pace increasing with Sierra's cry.

"Do it, Jaime. Please…make me come!"

Guiding Sierra to her, Jaime took her with abandon, pushing her tongue farther into slick warm flesh. She cried out Jaime's name. Her body throbbing against Jaime's tongue, her life force pulsed wildly with the urgency to explode. But it still wasn't enough. Sucking Sierra's heat, Jaime drove two fingers deep inside her, nearly lifting her out of the window.

"More, baby. Make me yours."

She wrapped her legs around Jaime's neck and gripped the window frame until her fingers turned white. She tried to match Jaime with every thrust of her hips but it wasn't enough. She wanted to be closer to her and longed for the connection she'd never experienced with another person. Moving to wrap her arms around Jaime's neck instead, she kissed Jaime and thrust into her hand, feeling the powerful orgasm beginning to swirl within.

"Damn, you're beautiful," Jaime said, breaking the kiss. "Look at me, baby. See my hunger for you when you come."

She locked eyes with Jaime and tried to speak, but the words left her in a rush. Her limbs went taut, her mind awash with bright light as the blinding orgasm crashed through her, wave upon wave of pure pleasure coursing through her body. As she trembled in Jaime's arms, she felt herself being placed on the bed. Jaime moved down her body, placing soft kisses first along her breasts, then down her abdomen. When soft lips encircled her clitoris, another wave crashed into her with bruising intensity.

"Oh my God." She gasped as Jaime feasted between her legs. She tried to tell her to stop, but her voice broke as a larger storm churned within, gathering strength. Her legs began to shake. The crescendo built as Jaime commanded her body like a captain would their vessel. Her feelings crested as the first warning spasms rolled through her, and just when she thought she'd succumbed to the sheer pleasure of it all, Jaime took her deeper, past reason, and inevitably over the edge.

"Let go, baby," Jaime said, her hand still buried deep inside her. When the spasms quieted to soft tremors, Jaime moved to recline along her length. "I've got you," Jaime whispered, placing soft kisses over her face.

"God, you're incredible. I think my bones melted," she said, still trying to catch her breath.

"Cold?" Jaime asked as she shivered.

"No. You?"

"Hot, actually."

"That you are." She forced Jaime onto her back and straddled her slim hips. Thrusting her wet center into her stomach, she marked Jaime's shirt with the remnants of her desire. Jaime unclasped Sierra's bra, licking her lips when Sierra's breasts were exposed.

"You're so fucking hot." Jaime tried to grab a swaying tip with her teeth but missed when Sierra pulled away.

"Out of your clothes. Now." She tugged at Jaime's T-shirt. "Your pants too." She didn't want to talk. She wanted to claim Jaime the way Jaime had claimed her.

Jaime raised her hips, removing every shred of clothing in record time, ignoring the twinge of unease born of too long without physical contact with someone else. She pulled Sierra back down on top of her, teasing Sierra's entrance with her fingertip. Sierra moaned.

"Oh no, you don't." Sierra grabbed her hands, pinning them expertly above her head.

"Baby, please. I'm dying here."

"Then maybe you need a little CPR." Sierra leaned forward and thrust her tongue into Jaime's mouth. Jaime wriggled beneath her but Sierra's position gave her the advantage. "I'm going to let your hands go, but no touching," Sierra said, sitting back on her heels.

"You can't expect me to lie here and watch?" Jaime asked, incredulous.

"Yes I can. But more important," Sierra nipped one of her nipples then the other, "I want you to feel."

It had been so long since she had allowed another woman to touch her she thought she might explode into a million pieces. She'd never wanted anyone to wield this kind of power over her—never wanted to be exposed in any way, even if there was the slightest possibility that she could end up getting hurt. Her father had taught her that emotions made people weak. She'd written a character that never allowed emotions to get in the way of her missions, no matter the cost to her sanity. But with Sierra's every touch and soft brush of lips, she was beginning to believe that not only did love make a person stronger, it made them feel invincible.

"Does this hurt?" Sierra asked as she traced the jagged tissue on her left side.

"No. I told you, when you touch me, I feel no pain."

Sierra reached between their bodies, taking Jaime's exposed clitoris between her fingers. "What do you feel now?"

She crushed the bedsheets in her hands, ripping them from their corners. She didn't know how much more of the teasing she could handle, and when Sierra pinched harder and tugged, she nearly rocketed off the bed. "Oh, God. Hurts so good. I need…"

"Me." Sierra pushed deep into her with one fluid motion and her body greedily engulfed her hand like rose petals closing during a heavy rain. She cried out, quickly flipping Sierra over to hover above her. She placed one leg between Sierra's, creating enough room to slip into her depths. As soon as the connection was made between their bodies, she tensed above Sierra and bore down hard onto her hand.

The contractions spread like wildfire between them, quickly engulfing them in a sensual heat. Within seconds they had immersed themselves completely, the inferno slowly dwindling to smoldering ashes, barely leaving them enough oxygen to speak.

"What…did you…do?" Sierra asked when she finally caught her breath.

"Me?" She gasped. "Jesus, baby. You wrecked me."

Sierra grinned against her sweaty neck, licking toward her ear. "You're a top. I like it."

"I'm so glad. But damn, I don't think I can walk."

"I'm sure you could, if I'd let you up."

"Let me?"

"Yes."

She kissed Sierra unhurriedly until the smoldering embers ignited once again. When she pulled back, the heat was evident in Sierra's smoky blue gaze. "And how do you plan to stop me?"

❖

Sierra woke the next morning, sensing Jaime's absence immediately. Her spot was still warm though, so she hadn't been gone that long. She was thankful for the reprieve and wondered if Jaime had left to avoid her or the conversation they needed to have. She should have been happy. She'd finally given in to her body's demand to have Jaime touch her, and Jaime didn't disappoint. Jaime was an amazing lover and she couldn't imagine anyone else taking her so forcefully but lovingly. But she couldn't trust the honesty in Jaime's touch or admit that she'd given Jaime her all. True, she'd had the most amazing three orgasms of her life but that had been simply a physical response to Jaime. Her mind, on the other hand, had erected an invisible force field around her heart. Since she couldn't trust Jaime's feelings or her own, she'd held a piece of herself back—guarded her heart from ever being hurt by the one person who'd always owned a piece of it.

As she lay there staring at the ceiling, she fought telling Jaime how she felt and wondered about the possibility of going back to just being friends. She rationalized that it would be best not to want Jaime anymore. But as her internal struggle raged she couldn't fight the fact that all she'd ever wanted was Jaime's touch. Jaime's words, her voice, her smell could intoxicate her more than any drug could. For once, part of her understood addiction and what effort it took to fight the craving for the one single thing that attached itself to every part of her being.

She gasped as she thought of Jaime's hands and how they'd touched every part of her body, recalled Jaime's lips, so soft and warm as they trailed kisses over every inch of her skin. Jaime had been a thorough lover. And as she thought about every touch, the cravings stirred once again.

Her skin began to prickle at the memory of the sudden change that had come over Jaime. The fire in Jaime's eyes and the hungry look had been intense and downright hot. She'd never experienced Jaime's aggressive side. Jaime had never been the aggressor and Sierra admitted that she loved every moment of it. Jaime had given her orgasm after swirling orgasm, and her body pushed limits that she never knew existed. If she accepted all of Jaime, would Jaime continually surprise her like this? All these unanswered questions. So much she didn't know and much left to be uncovered.

The unknown was what frightened her. Every day had been an unknown with Eric, and as she lay there thinking, she realized she couldn't drop the barriers she had erected around her heart because those shields were there for her own protection.

Jaime's admission last night had changed everything. She would have to tell Jaime soon and try to resist the temptation of sleeping with her again. They had only two more nights on the ship left, and no matter how much her body demanded Jaime, she would fight to not satisfy that thirst. She couldn't allow her hunger to overrule her better judgment, no matter how much her body demanded one more taste.

CHAPTER SIXTEEN

"Alex, look at me." Flynn begged, not caring if she sounded as vulnerable as she felt.

"I can't," Alex said, choking on her words.

Flynn placed her palm on Alex's cheek, using her thumb to wipe away the tears as they fell. "What hurts you so much?"

"Do you know what it does to me every time you leave, every time you accept another mission? I have no way of knowing whether you're alive or dead. Do you know I'd rather die than see you hurt? Without being able to touch you, to see you, I can't convince myself that you're not out there injured or, worse, dead. Sometimes when I touch you, I'm not even sure if you're real."

She pulled Alex close, wrapping her up in the safety of her arms. "I'm real, baby. Right here, flesh and blood. Feel me." She placed Alex's hand over her heart. "Let me prove it to you."

Alex grabbed her by the lapels, shaking her with anger. "Damn you, Flynn. Damn you for making me fall in love with you."

She kissed Alex soundly, lifting her into her arms and carrying her into the cabin surrounded by trees and shafts of moonlight. She couldn't let her go now, not without losing the will to live.

"I love you too, Alex. I think I always have. I was just too stupid to see it."

Alex placed her head onto Flynn's shoulder as a shudder tore through her body. "I can't do this with you, Flynn. I couldn't bear it if I woke up in the morning to find you gone."

She leaned forward to kiss a few of Alex's tears away before placing her gently onto the large oak-framed bed. She stripped naked before Alex, baring her body and soul. "When you wake up tomorrow morning, I'll be here," she said, lowering her body to rest on top of Alex's. "I promise."

"Not too bad, Flynn. I think we're onto something," Jaime murmured, hitting Save on the keyboard. Two solid hours of writing. Finally, Flynn had a path.

Since tiptoeing out of Sierra's room early that morning, she hadn't stopped writing. Darlene had left their cabin earlier than normal to meet some friends, allowing her the time she needed to get her thoughts down before they vanished. A few thousand words later, she couldn't believe her progress, not remembering a time in her life when the words had flowed so effortlessly. She knew the sudden breakthrough had more to do with the fact that she'd finally let her guard down and the world hadn't ended. Nor had she needed anything mind-altering, other than Sierra, to start writing again. This time it was all about being happy. Unfortunately it seemed that happiness would most likely be short-lived.

Last night in Sierra's arms she'd never felt so tranquil but alive at the same time. That sense of belonging was something she'd been missing in her life. Their connection was even stronger than when they were in school. But then sex did have a way of strengthening bonds. Those few incredible hours together were the most magical of Jaime's existence, and it had nearly killed her to walk out of that room before Sierra awoke. She'd scribbled a note for Sierra to come get her for breakfast in the morning in hopes that after last night's confession Sierra still wanted to see her.

She had wanted to be gone before Sierra woke up, afraid that seeing morning-after regret in Sierra's eyes would shatter her. She also needed a bit of space to get her own thoughts in order, and she couldn't do that with Sierra's scent and touch driving her crazy. Sierra had said that for one night she'd wanted to forget about the past. But what about the next morning? What did that mean for their future?

She should have asked that question before anything happened between them, but the need to have Sierra in her arms overshadowed all responsible thought. She'd lost count of how many times they'd made love. She had promised Sierra she could do short-term, pretend they had no past to worry about for one night. But then she had touched her, felt her soft skin under her fingertips, listened as she cried out, yielding her body to Jaime's touch. Sierra had calmed a part of her soul, and she'd never be the same, no matter what happened. Two days was all she had left to prove to Sierra that she could trust her touch, trust *her*. She'd have to do her damnedest to persuade her, especially since after that one glorious night she wanted a thousand more like it.

Before Sierra, writing had reminded her of her past. Sometimes the memories were so powerful, she couldn't write for weeks. But since Sierra had come back into her life, writing was not only fun again, she hungered for it. That morning, her writing was actually allowing her to forget about her past. It helped banish the thoughts of eventually explaining to Sierra how she could only solve her lifelong problem by living day to day.

But Sierra already knew that. She'd unfortunately experienced being with someone who struggled with addiction. Facing Sierra last night had been like living her worst nightmare. Admitting she couldn't be the person Sierra thought her to be, that she'd never be Sierra's hero, killed a small piece of her. Of course, who would ever see her as a hero? What a ridiculous notion since heroes didn't have weaknesses.

To know that someone had hurt Sierra both physically and emotionally made her want to strike out at them, and knowing that Sierra could lump her into the same category made her feel sick. Violence wasn't uncommon for people with addiction issues, but at least Jaime could always say she'd never mistreated anyone but herself. She had to stop thinking about Eric—about him touching Sierra, hurting her. At least the anger helped keep her mind clear. She'd need a clear head for the next few days. Those precious moments were all she had left before their fairy tale ended and she'd have to face an unknown future.

She looked around her empty cabin wishing she could talk to Darlene about everything before she left to hang out with Sierra for the day. But what could Darlene say that she didn't already know? She didn't need another lecture on how she should have told Sierra sooner. No, that would only make the pain worse and make her see what a fool she'd been, not to mention give Darlene the chance to say I told you so. Unable to ignore her rumbling stomach any longer, she decided to grab a quick bite to eat, since it didn't look like Sierra was going to show. Not wanting to think about what that meant, she grabbed her room key and reached for the door handle just as Darlene pushed her way in, followed closely by Sierra.

"Hey," she said, surprised.

"Hey." Sierra gave her a quick peck on the cheek as Darlene stood in the doorway wearing a Cheshire-cat grin.

"What are you both doing here?" *Uh-oh. This can't be good.*

"I ran into Darlene on the way to come find you," Sierra said. "She was just explaining that you were in one of your creative modes. Is this a good time?"

"It's fine." S*hit!* She could only imagine what else Darlene had said.

"Yeah, because if you want us to leave, we can," Darlene said, her grin turning evil. "I wanted to talk with Sierra anyway. She was catching me up on *current* events."

"Really?" She glanced at Sierra, who smiled sheepishly and blushed. "How current?"

"Nothing too specific," Sierra said, sitting on her lap. "She wanted details but I only threw her tidbits. Stop frowning."

"How small were these tidbits?"

"Sierra told me I could only ask her two questions, and I agreed," Darlene said.

"Which were?"

"Where and, in one word, what was involved," Sierra said.

"No way." She blushed. "You didn't?"

"Yes...sorry!" Sierra squealed as Jaime tickled her.

"Jesus, I can't believe you two."

"Don't worry. I didn't give away any of the gory details, although I did tell her you were spectacular." She tickled Sierra again until her squirming ended with her falling onto the floor. "Stop! I give already."

"And just what are you willing to give?" She hoisted Sierra into her lap and placed a soft kiss behind her ear.

"Helloooooooo…I'm still in the room." Darlene rolled her eyes.

"Whoops," Sierra said, putting a finger over Jaime's lips to halt the next kiss. "Sorry, Darlene. That reminds me. Darlene and I were wondering if you had plans today?"

"I don't think so, why?"

"Well, we dock in Grand Cayman in an hour and were wondering if you'd consider going snorkeling with us."

The room spun and she clutched the bed to stop the dizzying effects. She'd almost forgotten about the snorkeling idea since she'd literally been so wrapped up in Sierra the last few days. Did she possess the courage to do it?

"Jaime, it's okay," Sierra said, holding on tight to her hand. "Darlene and I discussed this. We don't have to go if you don't want to."

She felt Sierra wipe away tears that she just now realized she'd shed. How could she go back into the water after all this time? She wanted to overcome one of her greatest fears but didn't know if she was strong enough, especially while worrying about their relationship. Some hero she was. "I'd like to try. I'm scared though."

"Darlene, could you give us a minute?" Sierra asked.

"Sure. I'll be right outside."

"Jaime, look at me." Sierra tugged on her hand. "Everything's okay. Breathe."

She wrapped her arms around Sierra's neck and placed her head on Sierra's shoulder, waiting for the tears to subside. Sierra rubbed her back, but the touch seemed strictly friendly in nature. The lack of warmth in Sierra's touch intensified the lump in her throat. She pulled away.

"I understand this is a huge step for you," Sierra said. "I promise, if you do this, I'll be there the whole time."

She rubbed a shaky arm across her face. "I'm counting on it," she said, not having the energy to wish for more.

❖

The sun was at its zenith when the group adjusted their fins and donned their masks, wading out into the clear blue water. The warmth of the tropical seas felt very different than the cold waters Jaime had always surfed in. She gazed at the wide expanse of ocean as her heart thudded wildly. She tried to find the saliva needed to spit into her mask, but her mouth was as dry as the desert in July.

"You doing okay?" Sierra placed her hand on her shoulder.

"Yeah." Her voice cracked. She inhaled deeply, the salt from the sea air tickling her nose. She put her mask on, blowing through the snorkel to clear the water. "I'm good. Really. Just…stay close."

"You don't have to worry about *that*. I'm not leaving you for a second. Ready?"

She gave Sierra the universal thumbs-up sign before submerging. As the salt water pooled around her, she willed herself not to panic when it rendered her weightless. Taking slow gulps of air she tried to relax as she nervously scanned her surroundings. She pictured being a piece of bait clinging to a hook, afraid of what might jump out of the darkness and take a bite. Why had she agreed to this insanity? Just when she thought she couldn't find the courage to move, Sierra grabbed one of her hands and she propelled herself forward.

Drifting atop the water like two floating logs, they watched as schools of tropical fish floated all around them. She constantly searched her flank for anything out of the ordinary, but every so often, Sierra squeezed her hand, letting her know she wasn't alone. The simple act anchored her, and for the first time in a long time, she didn't feel like she was adrift in the sea that was her life.

Darlene eventually caught up to them, after making some lame excuse about getting a better look at a stingray. Jaime loved her for it and knew it was Darlene's way of granting them space. She hadn't found the chance to talk to Darlene about the Sierra situation since all three of them had left together that morning. She'd hoped to find a few minutes alone with her before they went snorkeling, but hadn't.

As they spent the next hour enjoying the many colors of the coral reef and the large groups of sea turtles that inhabited the area, she contemplated how to tell Sierra she wanted more out of their relationship, that one night would never be enough. As the day progressed and Sierra became more indifferent toward her, her apprehension grew.

Finally, after two hours in the water, they made their way back to shore. She'd thought that overcoming her biggest fear would have lifted the weight from her shoulders, and partly it had. But even though she was proud of herself, she wasn't happy about the distance that had seemed to stretch wider between her and Sierra over the course of the day.

"That was so much fun," Sierra said, towel-drying her hair.

"Yeah, it really was. Thanks to you both." She grabbed them and pulled them into a bear hug.

"You don't need to thank us, sweetie, but I'm glad you enjoyed it," Sierra said, kissing her chastely. "I need to go find the little-girls' room. Be back in a sec."

She stared after Sierra, jumping when Darlene swatted her with her towel.

"I assume you told her," Darlene said.

"Yes, and I don't know what to make of it." She kept her eyes glued to the door just in case Sierra appeared.

"Well, don't keep me in suspense."

"She said she wanted to keep it casual."

"Ouch." Darlene grimaced. "And how do you feel about that?"

"How do you think I feel about it?" she answered sarcastically. "I'm kinda not liking it." She pulled on a dry shirt with a scowl. She needed to have this conversation with Darlene, but coming on the heels of going back in the water, she didn't feel like it.

"Then why don't you tell her that?"

"Novel idea. Gee, why didn't I think of that?"

"Jaime," Darlene said. "You're being an ass."

"Sorry," she mumbled, but the whole Sierra situation was really starting to get to her. All day she'd tried to touch Sierra, lean forward to kiss her. And what happened? Sierra shied away, barely looking at her. She hated the barrier between them, which confused her. When Sierra had shown up at her room that morning, she'd been relaxed and playful. But the wall now marked the end of that mood, and she didn't know what had put it up.

She wanted to tear it down, rip away what was really preventing Sierra from taking that chance with her. But except for trivial conversation, Sierra wouldn't talk about what had happened between them last night. The thought depressed her. "I'm trying to get her to open up to me, but I haven't had any luck."

"Think she'll eventually come around?"

"God, I hope so," she said, but stopped talking when Sierra finally emerged from the bathroom, looking at them strangely.

"Hey, what did I miss?" Sierra looked curiously back and forth between them.

"Nothing," she said quickly. "Darlene and I couldn't agree on where to go for lunch. That's all." She discreetly threw Darlene a warning look, letting her know she'd better play along.

"Is that it?"

Sierra looked skeptical, but Jaime gave her one of her award-winning smiles. "Yep. We were thinking Mexican. How does that sound?"

"Perfect."

Darlene shook her head and walked away. Perfect wasn't really the word for it.

CHAPTER SEVENTEEN

Jaime sat across from Sierra inside the packed buffet, watching her consume a healthy plate of mixed dinner items from the many options offered. Normally after the kind of intense day she'd had, the smell of steak, shrimp, and potatoes au gratin would have tickled her taste buds to the point she'd be a salivating mess. But after the way her day with Sierra had gone, she didn't have an appetite.

She'd never been able to eat when she was nervous. When they'd decided to skip going to the dining room that night she'd actually been relieved. She had no desire to sit around with Darlene and a bunch of their other former classmates and pretend everything was great, because it wasn't. She'd hoped they could skip dinner altogether and go for a walk to get things out in the open between them, but Sierra said that her growling stomach wasn't leaving her much choice in the matter.

"Aren't you hungry?" Sierra asked, finishing the last bite of potatoes. "You haven't touched anything on your plate."

"Not really. Guess I'm still full from lunch." She lied, not wanting to tell Sierra that the massive burrito she'd eaten earlier felt like a rock in the pit of her stomach.

"Jaime, that was hours ago. How about a little something? Maybe some soup. For me."

She grimaced. Sierra always used the "for-me" trick when she wanted her to do something. She'd used the famous ploy when they were teenagers too, and it'd worked every time. The last time Sierra had asked her to do something out of guilt, she had stood in the corner of one of Sierra's high-school friend's homes for hours while Sierra made out with Charlie Frisk during some stupid birthday party. Reluctantly she downed a few spoonfuls of her French onion soup that had turned cold long ago.

"Come on," Sierra said, rising. "I can see you're only humoring me. Let's get outta here."

Grateful, she set down her spoon and followed Sierra to the ship's library. She'd hoped Sierra would have wanted to talk back in her room, but the growing distance between them all day made being in public an obvious choice. At ten at night the library was empty, so each of them sat in a high-back leather chair that faced the open ocean. The nautical-themed room was stacked floor to ceiling with leather-bound books. The musty smell of those old books had always attracted her, and she wasn't sure whether it was the author or the romantic in her that made her feel that way.

"Thinking about writing?" Sierra asked.

"Actually, yes, in a way. I love libraries. How did you guess?"

"Duh, you're an author," Sierra said, making her laugh softly. "What writer doesn't like books?"

"I see your point."

She tried to twine her fingers through Sierra's, but as soon as their hands touched, Sierra discreetly pulled away and pretended to concentrate on the shelves of books against the far wall. When Sierra asked her a question about which classic was her favorite, she tried to swallow the ball of fire in her throat, having a hard time keeping the disappointment out of her voice. Sierra did look at her then, and the mask of restraint she'd put in place all day slipped slightly.

"Jaime," Sierra whispered. "Please, stop looking at me like that."

"I can't help it," she said desperately. "This distance between us is killing me. I can't describe it any other way."

"Please, let's not do this."

"Do what? Tell you that last night was the most amazing night of my life?"

"It was for me too, but things are different now. Can't we have a good time, enjoy each other's company? Let's face it, in a few days this cruise is going to end—"

"No!" she said quickly, fearing Sierra's next words. "I can't think about that. I refuse to think about anything except how happy and terrified you make me all at the same time. I look at you and sometimes I don't believe you're real. And then you touch me and every one of my senses comes alive. God! I'm not making any sense." She choked, tears falling down her face.

Either her confession or her tears made Sierra spring out of her chair and pull her into her arms. It didn't matter. All that mattered was that, for the first time that day, Sierra's touch didn't feel hesitant and her kiss was unrestrained. Jaime's blood boiled and flowed like molten lava through her veins. Her skin tingled and wetness pooled between her thighs. She groaned as she pulled Sierra closer.

"God, please, Sierra. Let me touch you. You're all I need.*"*

Sierra nodded wordlessly. Any further discussion between them would have to wait.

❖

Sierra closed the door behind them and they stared at one other hesitantly. Jaime didn't move and looked as nervous as Sierra felt.

"I'm shaking," Jaime admitted.

"Here, let me help you." She placed her hands on Jaime's hips, watching her hazy emerald eyes as they darkened to evergreen. Grabbing the hem of Jaime's T-shirt, she lifted it over her head as Jaime stared at her breathlessly. Jaime never moved, allowing her to do whatever she wished.

"I don't think I could ever get tired of staring at your body," she said, leaning forward to lick the thin sheen of sweat from Jaime's neck. She unbuttoned Jaime's jeans at the same time she pushed them down her hips for Jaime to step out of them.

"I'm so glad."

Jaime tilted her head for a kiss as Sierra pushed her tongue urgently into Jaime's mouth. Jaime grunted when she bit down, the fight for dominance ending when Jaime pinned her against the stateroom door. Her shorts and top disappeared, and she reached for Jaime's hands to place them on her breasts.

"Touch me," she moaned, her legs threatening to buckle as Jaime pinched her nipples into two painful tips. She ached for Jaime to take one of them into her mouth, almost pleaded as Jaime held her steady with one leg between her parted thighs. She thrashed her head from side to side. Too many sensations. Too many emotions all at once for her to sort them out. When Jaime placed one hand between her legs she was seconds from losing it. "Not yet. Please, Jaime. Don't make me come yet."

Jaime quickly spun her around as they toppled onto the bed with her on top, one of her legs falling perfectly between Jaime's. She moaned when she felt Jaime's arousal, warm and wet against her thigh.

"You're so hard," she said, sliding her thigh along Jaime's clit. Jaime arched below her, using her body to apply more pressure.

"Only for you." Jaime panted. "I was wrong about not being hungry."

"Oh, how so?" She took one of Jaime's nipples between her teeth and Jaime hissed.

"I wasn't before. Guess I'll have to satisfy my appetite by eating you instead."

"Feast away."

She offered her neck to Jaime, moaning with every gentle nip and pass of teeth and tongue. A trail of goose bumps covered her flesh. She was breathless. "God, I'm almost there."

"I know. I can feel you." Jaime grasped her hips, motioning her forward, then positioned her directly above her head, guiding her down into her waiting mouth.

"Feels so good...Oh!" She framed her sex, giving Jaime full access to whatever she desired.

"Please..." She begged, rocking her hips. "Suck me. I need you to."

Jaime moaned in response, taking the tense shaft between her teeth. Jaime tugged gently as Sierra cried out and shifted forward, bracing herself against the headboard for support. Jaime let her set the pace, and she took advantage of it, slowing down and speeding up, drawing out her orgasm as long as she could.

She squirmed above Jaime as waves of her rising passion thrummed powerfully against her walls. The pressure built deep within, and with every talented stroke of Jaime's tongue, her restraint eroded like sands in heavy surf. She wanted the exquisite feeling to last but her body had other ideas.

"Yesohyes!" She drove hard against Jaime's mouth, riding out her orgasm as the shock waves reverberated throughout her body. As the last spasms faded like the tides, she slumped boneless into Jaime's waiting arms, gasping from what little oxygen seemed to remain inside the room.

"Now that was my idea of a private excursion. All that exercise and I didn't even have to leave the boat." Jaime panted, holding on tight to her limp body.

Hearing pure need in Jaime's voice, she quickly slid between Jaime's legs. She nipped at the tender skin just below Jaime's navel, enjoying the sounds that reverberated from her. "As you can see, I had other activities planned."

"Really?" Jaime gasped when Sierra dipped her tongue lower. "Are all these activities private?"

"Damn straight they are," she said, jealousy streaking down her spine like lightning on a hot Midwestern night. "Unless you have any objections, in which case we might have a problem." She bit the inside of Jaime's thigh, making her jump.

"No…no problem…Jesus!"

Jaime groaned as she stroked her clit with one long, slow stroke after another. The teasing continued until Jaime whimpered something unintelligible. The sight of Jaime naked and sprawled out above her, exposed and open, made her want things she couldn't put words to. But she had to push those things from her mind. She didn't dare dream of more, not when those dreams would eventually lead to heartache.

Taking Jaime firmly between her lips, she sucked, drawing a hoarse shout from her. Body bowed with a translucent sheen of sweat, Jaime finally broke. Her body shook uncontrollably until Sierra milked every last tremor from her body. She glanced up Jaime's long torso, not remembering having seen anyone more awe-inspiring than Jaime as she lay basking in the afterglow of their lovemaking.

"You're amazing," Jaime said between shallow breaths.

She smiled, resting her body lengthwise with her head on Jaime's shoulder while Jaime reclined on the bed with her back against the headboard. "Me? I think you hold the title on that one, stud."

"Is that so?" Jaime positioned Sierra between her legs so that Sierra's back was to her front. She slid her hand down the front of Sierra's body, burying her hand deep between Sierra's legs. "Then I want another chance to live up to my expectations."

Sierra didn't think she could become so aroused again so fast, but when she glanced down to find Jaime's hand disappearing deep inside her with each thrust, all thought fled. She laid her head back against Jaime's shoulder, crying out when Jaime used her free hand to pinch her nipple into a stone-hard peak. The twin sensations, combined with Jaime's wetness coating her body from behind, pushed her body to the brink. "More, Jaime. Fill me up."

Jaime surged against her, her cries filling Sierra's head as her fingers filled Sierra's body. Jaime grew impossibly hard, rubbing her need against the cleft in Sierra's ass. Sierra clamped down hard over Jaime's hand, pushing Jaime's fingers more forcefully against her painfully rigid clitoris. The motion slammed her body tighter between Jaime's legs, and as her body poised for release, Jaime delivered the final stroke that made them both tumble into orgasm.

❖

Jaime held Sierra as she lay fast asleep in her arms. She softly kissed the top of Sierra's head, watching the orange and red hues of the early morning break through the darkness. Unlike the rest of the past week, she wasn't looking forward to the new day. She thought it ironic that a week ago she didn't want to go on this cruise. Now, as Sierra lay snoring softly in her arms, she couldn't imagine wanting to be anywhere else.

She hadn't planned to make love with Sierra again. Of course, touching Sierra was all she could think about, but Sierra's distant behavior had made her think she'd never get the chance. She'd intended to lay her heart on the line, to tell Sierra that she wanted a chance at a relationship with her and to beg, if that's what it took, for the chance. But as soon as she began to tell Sierra how she felt, she'd crumbled. She hurt in some deep place that only Sierra knew how to access. As soon as Sierra had moved into her arms, she'd forgotten all about her intentions.

Struggling to take a deep breath, she tried to calm her pounding heart. What scared her more than anything was the unknown. Would Sierra understand or care about what she'd gone through to get to this point in her life? Would Sierra believe her when she told her that their relationship was more important than anything else in the world? Did Sierra have the faith or the ability to trust her after everything she'd suffered in the past? She sure hoped so.

She couldn't contain the tears that coursed down her cheeks. If only she hadn't been surfing that day or if she'd only been strong enough to fight the pain while still in the hospital, she wouldn't have anything to taint their relationship.

She wiped at her tear-stained cheeks with the sheet, careful not to wake Sierra. Damn it, why couldn't she have been strong enough? What had made her so weak that she'd nearly destroyed her life for pills? But of course, she'd always known that answer. Strength and courage had never been her strong suit. She wrote about a hero, one she dreamt of being in her everyday life. But heroes didn't cave when things got tough. They only became stronger, pushed past their pain, and, well, sucked it up. As Sierra stirred, she realized she was going to have to dig deep to find that courage. Sierra made her want to be stronger—made her want to face her shortcomings. She had realized long ago that pills were nothing more than an excuse to mask her physical and emotional pain. Having Sierra in her arms made her look at the world in a whole new light, and she vowed that if Sierra could ever forgive her, she'd do everything in her power to never hide anything from her again.

"Hey," Sierra said groggily. "What time is it?"

"Time for breakfast." Her voice sounded rough.

"You okay?"

"Yeah, fine. Allergies are acting up, I guess." *Yeah, lie to her some more. Great idea.*

"You sure?"

"Positive. Come on." Jaime climbed out of bed and extended her hand. "Let's take a shower and go get some grub. I'm starving."

"I bet. You didn't touch dinner last night."

Sierra placed her hand in hers, and she could swear by the hungry look on Sierra's face that she too felt the electricity pass between them.

"Not to mention," Sierra said, throwing her arms around her neck, their naked bodies wound closely together, "you did get quite a workout last night."

"That I did," she said darkly, staring at Sierra's lips. "And I have to tell you, I'm kinda getting worked up again."

Sierra grabbed her hand and placed it between her legs. She held Jaime's hand hostage between her thighs. "I was hoping."

She struggled for breath as Sierra rode her hand vigorously, throwing her head back as her orgasm consumed her. She'd never felt so humbled in another person's presence and would have dropped to her knees and begged for Sierra's forgiveness, if Sierra hadn't dropped to her knees and taken Jaime's clit in her mouth before she had the chance.

She leaned against the wall, spreading her legs wide as Sierra kneeled before her with Jaime's hands wrapped up in her hair. The feel of Sierra's mouth on her consumed her and she let it, even if the flame devoured her entirely.

CHAPTER EIGHTEEN

The Grand Ballroom was packed for the last dinner seating of the cruise. Jaime sat close to Sierra, her leg tingling where Sierra's hand rested possessively on her leg. She'd been sipping her coffee as Sierra talked animatedly with one of their classmates at a nearby table.

Darlene glared at her the entire time, especially since they'd had a heated discussion in their cabin before dinner. The argument had ended with Jaime storming out. She wasn't in the mood to listen to how she was hurting Sierra further by not telling her exactly how she felt. Of course she couldn't stay mad at Darlene, who was afraid she would get hurt. She loved her for caring, but sometimes Darlene just needed to back off.

Laughter echoed in the large room, the festivities slowly beginning to die down. Surprisingly, she was having a good time. In the last few days, she'd actually exchanged e-mail addresses with quite a few old classmates, promising to keep in touch after the cruise ended. If it hadn't been for Darlene pushing her to go and Sierra striking up many of the conversations, she would have missed out on a lot of possible friendships—another positive to having Sierra in her life.

"What would you like to do now?" Sierra said as Jaime shook their waiter's hand and tipped him handsomely for his excellent service.

"I thought a walk up top might be nice." She held her arm out for Sierra to take. *I can't prolong this any longer.*

Sierra linked arms with her as they rode the elevator to the top deck of the ship. She propped herself against the railing, pulling Sierra close. Burying her face in Sierra's hair, she savored the familiar scent of coconut-and-lime shampoo.

"Cold?" Sierra asked when Jaime shivered.

"No. It's something else." She placed Sierra at arm's length and looked deeply into her eyes. "I wanted to talk about what happens afterward."

"Oh…that." Sierra moved away and rested her back against the railing. "I thought we agreed to keep things simple."

"No, *we* didn't. You said that. I want more."

"How much more?" Sierra whispered, looking at her feet.

"I want the happy ending."

"I can't." Sierra choked. "And you know why. The risk. It's too much like with Eric."

"I am not Eric," she said defiantly. "Please don't punish me for his sins. I have enough to repent for on my own."

"I understand that, but I'm not ready for more. Maybe we should go back to the way things were?" Sierra glanced at her almost pleadingly.

Usually she could find solace in Sierra's blue eyes, but she swore she caught a flicker of fear, or was that the reflection of her own pain? "What do you mean, like friends?"

"Exactly." For the first time, Sierra looked hopeful. "We'll exchange numbers, e-mails. Maybe meet for dinner occasionally."

She couldn't believe what she was hearing. Sierra had to be joking. Had she just suggested they should pretend that nothing had happened between them? Was she that easy for Sierra to forget?

"No." She approached Sierra and grabbed her by the arms. "Damn it, look at me! I could never go back. I don't want to be your friend or some occasional fuck buddy. Not after touching you. How could you ask that of me? I want a chance at a relationship. You…me… making a life together. I'm asking for that chance."

She was relieved to find that asking for what she wanted, demanded, had been easier than she'd anticipated. Once she'd started to speak, the words poured from her like they had been since she'd begun writing again. She wouldn't be afraid to ask Sierra for anything anymore, to plead if she had to. Not with the stakes so high. Tired of proving herself, she placed all her chips on the line. It was everything or nothing.

She could see Sierra struggling, the confusion and sadness in her eyes showing her inner turmoil. Sierra finally looked up and met her eyes. "I'm sorry. I can't."

She staggered back as if struck. Her whole body trembled. "Are you sure?" she asked, her throat tight.

"Yes. I'm sorry. I just can't take the chance."

She leaned forward to kiss Sierra. "I guess this is good-bye then." She shook her head and stepped back. Damn, it hurt. "I wish I could change your mind, but I won't push you. Take care of yourself." She walked away, leaving Sierra, and her chance at love, behind.

God, grant me the serenity to accept the things I cannot change.
The words echoed like a mantra inside her head. She had to keep moving, afraid that if she turned around that she'd run back to Sierra and accept the offer of a casual friendship. Trying to steady herself, she placed her hand over her chest in an effort to massage away the building pressure that made her chest ache and every breath unbearable. For the second time in her life, accepting the things she couldn't change seemed like a sick joke. She cursed God. An immortal being that believed in love and forgiveness could not possibly exist, especially not after tonight.

Courage to change the things I can.
Courage, yeah, like that had helped. She angrily swiped at her tears. Finding the strength to spill her guts had backfired. But what had angered her most and given her the much-needed strength to walk away was Sierra's easy dismissal of what they had shared. Fuck buddies or friends, seriously? After the long nights of making love and sharing a piece of themselves with each other, it was unimaginable to think that Sierra could act like it had meant nothing. To even suggest it was equivalent to taking a dagger to the heart.

And the wisdom to know the difference.

Wisdom. Hell, there was something she could use right now. She wished her sponsor was accessible by phone. She could use someone else's opinion of what she could have done differently. Of course, if she needed someone to list her faults there was always Darlene. Probably not a wise decision since she wasn't in the mood for a lecture.

Refusing to go back to her room, she walked the ship for hours, scanning ahead to make sure she wouldn't run into Sierra. At least after tomorrow she'd never have to worry about that again. The top deck was quiet at the late hour, similar to the night she and Sierra had confessed their feelings for one another. Exhaustion overcame her and she sank to her knees, allowing her heavy sobs to wrack her body. Eventually she clawed at the closest railing and managed to get back to her feet. Every muscle in her body was tired, and just when she'd thought her night couldn't get any worse a distinct voice called out to her from behind.

"Well, looky looky here," Bo bellowed. "Your girl kick you out of the bedroom for poor performance?"

She stiffened, not in the mood for Bo's razzing after the night she'd had. As he moved closer, she was surprised his breath didn't give her a contact high, the strong stench of Jack Daniels repulsive. She wanted to take a step back but nothing but open ocean lay behind her. "Give it a rest and get lost, Tyson."

"Make me. You're always all talk. Why don't you do something about it this time," he said, menacingly poking a pudgy finger into her chest.

Suddenly she forgot Bo was twice her weight, forgot he was some poor drunk sap who didn't know he was prodding a wounded animal. In her anger, she associated Bo with Eric, Sierra's ex, the person who had wronged Sierra and made it impossible for her to give them both a chance. She cocked her fist, about to hit him, and then felt…nothing. For some reason her legs didn't want to support her weight. Darkness eclipsed her just before the world exploded in a mixture of white light and blinding pain, and she felt like she was kneeling but she wasn't sure.

In a distant corner of her mind she heard screams, male voices moving closer, but she couldn't see their faces—couldn't see anything at all. The surface beneath her cheek felt cool. Sound faded until she was suffused in peace. Funny, all the pain was gone. Thankful for the brief respite, she closed her eyes and succumbed to the darkness.

❖

Jaime tried to open her eyes—tried to take a deep breath. Every inhalation was like swallowing fire. She could hear someone talking, but it sounded like they were underwater—distorted and far away. Was she drowning? She gripped the heavily starched sheets below her. Nope. She was definitely lying on a bed—a very uncomfortable bed.

"Don't move," a comforting but commanding voice said.

"Who are…" She winced at the brain-shatteringly bright light. She tried to sit up. *Whoa, bad idea.* "Is the room supposed to be moving like that?"

Someone laughed. "Normally, no, but not surprising with the concussion you most likely have. Now lie still."

"No choice. Feel like crap." She collapsed onto the sheets, groaning as every cell in her body screamed out in pain. "Jesus, what the hell happened to me?"

"You were beat up."

"By what? Feels like a couple of dolphins have been playing volleyball with my head."

The woman smiled and pulled out what appeared to be some kind of ship's document. "Actually, the report says your assailant was a white male, approximately six-three and about two-eighty. Ring any bells?"

Jaime nodded, the motion making her want to vomit. "Yeah, my bell got rung all right." She gingerly turned her head to take a good look at the tall, exotic-looking brunette wearing a lab coat and scrutinizing her every move. "Are you my doctor?"

"Yes. And now that you're awake, I need to ask you a few questions." The doctor removed what looked like a pen from her pocket and shined light into Jaime's eyes. She winced and looked away. "Don't have to ask if that bothered you. How's the headache?"

"Manageable, but I'm more tired than anything else."

"Do you feel nauseous?"

"No."

"Dizzy?"

"At first but not now."

The doctor's face took on a serious expression as she pulled a stool closer to Jaime's bedside. "I don't think your injuries are life threatening, but I'd like to keep you overnight for observation. Your ribs are bruised and you possibly have a few fractures. You're going to need to be checked regularly and awoken frequently. It's a precaution in case you have a concussion, which I'm thinking is likely. You'll be very sore tomorrow but you'll pull through."

Oh, she'd pull through easily. Life wouldn't make things that easy for her. She welcomed the pain, since it made her concentrate on something else besides losing Sierra. She needed out of that room though. Since her accident, she didn't like any type of hospital settings. They brought up too many painful memories and she'd suffered enough for one night. Besides, she was upset, her side hurt like hell, and the lights were really pissing her off. Her headache was escalating by the second, and the more coherent she became the more she realized her anxiety had nothing to do with the room's poor lighting. "Thanks for the offer, Doc, but I can take care of myself."

"Hold on. I don't think—"

A loud commotion came from the other side of the infirmary door. Jaime smiled as the familiar voice escalated, even though the pain in her jaw increased the throbbing in her temples tenfold.

"What the hell happened?" Darlene asked as she pulled away from one of the ship's crew members and barged through the door wearing a T-shirt and a pair of pajama bottoms with frogs on them.

"Darlene, calm down," she said.

"Calm down? I get a phone call that someone beat you up and you're in the infirmary at two in the morning, and you want me to calm down?"

"Yes. I'm fine. Sorry they woke you."

"Jaime," Darlene said, placing her hand on Jaime's jaw and inspecting her injuries. "Who did this?"

"Bo *fucking* Tyson. Who else?" Jaime explained through gritted teeth.

"What did he hit you with?"

"First his fist then his boot," the doctor interjected. "Of course that's according to witnesses. The injuries coincide with their details."

"And where is psycho boot-kicker now?" Darlene asked the doctor.

"They've arrested him. He'll be turned over to the authorities when we dock tomorrow."

"No. I won't press charges."

"What!" Darlene said as the doctor raised a curious eyebrow but didn't speak. "Those injuries to your face must be worse than they look."

"Doesn't feel that bad." She placed her hand over her cheek. Yeah, it was warm and it hurt a little, but she suspected a little bruising at most. "Hand me a mirror, Darlene?"

"Jaime, maybe you should wait. Let's see what Doc has to say."

"Darlene, please."

Reluctantly Darlene held up the mirror and Jaime saw her injuries for the first time. So many colors surrounded her left eye she looked like she'd gone ten rounds with a boxer and lost. She had a laceration on the tip of her chin and a welt covering her right cheek. "Fuck!"

"Exactly." Darlene put the mirror down. "Now will you press charges?"

"No, because my decision has nothing to do with my injuries."

"Then what, because I'm outta the loop here."

"Darlene," she said, covering her eyes. God, it hurt to talk. "I tried to hit him first. I deserve this."

"You're taking responsibility for this? I will not allow you to stick up for that gay-bashing asshole. And where is Sierra? Does she know about this?"

"My choice," she said, suddenly very tired. She ignored the Sierra question. There'd be time for that later. "Can I go back to my room now?"

"Don't know." Darlene glanced at the doctor. "Doc?"

"I'll be okay with it if you follow my list of instructions to the letter. Otherwise, no deal. And if she has any symptoms…throwing up…dizziness…anything, you call me immediately."

"No problem," Darlene said, helping her to her feet.

"Would you like something for the pain?" the doctor asked before they left.

"No," she said, even though she'd sell her soul to make all the pain go away, especially the emotional pain. "Thanks, Doc."

They stepped into the hallway as Darlene wrapped an arm around her waist. "You gonna make it?"

That was a loaded question. "Yeah, just get me outta here. I wanna go home."

CHAPTER NINETEEN

Flynn woke to the sounds of birds chirping outside the cabin window. She blinked a few times to clear her head, taking a second to orient herself. Stretching like a Bengal cat after a long nap, she glanced at the clock. Six solid hours of sleep—an oddity for her. Not only was it the best night of sleep in her life, but she felt refreshed, renewed. Nothing could compare to having Alex in her arms. Nothing. Vivid images of Alex surrendering to her touch and calling out her name stirred her. Just thinking about Alex's knowing hands and soft brush of lips across her clitoris made her hard again. They'd made love throughout the night, and after the third orgasm she'd lost count. Recalling Alex's unique taste caused Flynn to reach for her. But as her hand came in contact with the cold, empty space next to her on the bed, she crushed the sheets below as panic rose inside her. "Alex?" she said, sitting up. "Alex!"

Alarm and something she couldn't name drove her through the empty cabin, pulling open every door, every window. Not a shred of evidence existed of their one night of passion. Nothing that could assure her that Alex had been there with her and she'd been real. Pushing her way through the door out into the cutting January morning, she stood still for a second as the gravity of her situation set in. Three feet of snow had gathered where Alex's car used to be.

Alex was gone. And she'd been gone for a while.

Her hand trembled as she reached awkwardly behind her for the rocker on the porch. She buried her face in her hands, the tears falling.

The temperature was below freezing outside, but the bitter cold couldn't match the void in her heart. For the first time in her life, she had stayed with a woman overnight, but this time she had awakened to an empty bed.

Standing on wobbly legs, she opened the door to stare dispassionately at the empty room. Alex had to be somewhere and she'd never give up until she was found. No one made her feel the way Alex could. No one made her want things she'd never considered before. When she found Alex, she would tell her all that and more. She would hide nothing from her. Her heart would be an open book. She just hoped Alex would open up too.

With an unsteady hand, she picked up her cell phone and dialed a familiar number. It took three rings for the person on the other end to answer.

"Agent 2261. Connect me to extension 4211."

"I'm sorry, ma'am. That extension is no longer in service," the voice responded respectfully.

"As of when?" she asked hoarsely.

"As of an hour ago, ma'am. Ms Chambers is no longer with the company."

The phone fell from her hand, shattering as it hit the wooden floor.

Jaime punched Save on her computer, wiping away the tears. She'd locked herself away for the past few months, refusing to emerge until she'd made her peace with Flynn's character.

Two months had passed since the cruise, two months since she'd touched Sierra. She had left the boat the day after the attack without seeing her, though plenty of people stopped her to comment on the situation with Bo Tyson. She had left them behind as quickly as possible, unwilling to chance Sierra seeing the mess her face was in.

She'd spent a majority of her days since either sitting in front of the computer writing or working out in her weight room. Physically she was in the best shape of her life. But her heart was torn apart. It hadn't found a steady rhythm since she and Sierra had parted. She'd had a lot of time to think, and she'd never blame Sierra for her decision. Barely being able to live with her own choices after everything that had happened, how could she have expected Sierra to be with her?

Most days she sat around the house wishing things could have been different. She'd lost weight and ate only for survival. Sleeping was rare. Nothing excited her any longer. All she had was her writing, but even that couldn't assuage the mind-numbing ache she'd experienced since she'd lost Sierra.

Darlene had called her numerous times since they returned, and most of their conversations revolved around trying to coax her to hook up with one of her former lovers—anything to help get her mind off Sierra. As if it would be that easy. When that didn't work, Darlene tried to get her out of the house for dinner, but she always refused, explaining that she just wanted to be left alone. All she'd ever wanted was Sierra. Too bad she blew it.

As days turned into weeks, she morphed into a shadow of the person she used to be. She'd rattle along the halls at night, like a ghost lost between worlds. Nothing seemed real any longer. Some days she even questioned if her time with Sierra had been real. Those magical moments felt more like dreams. But if they were dreams, she would drift back to sleep and find a way back to them. These were the thoughts that scared her most, the ones that made her crave an escape. They were dangerous thoughts for one who used to walk among the darkness. But she refused to break another promise again, whether to herself or someone else. She'd rather die in tremendous pain than to ever have to endure the hurt and disapproval on Sierra's face that she witnessed their final night together, even if she never saw her again.

Reaching into her desk drawer she pulled out a picture. The images staring back at her brought a smile to her face, even though the happy memories caused her unbearable sadness. The picture of their special prom night was now her only link to the past. "I miss you so damn much," she murmured, kissing Sierra's picture. She placed it back into the drawer, unable to stare at it for more than a few minutes at a time. That day seemed like an eternity ago, and it might as well have been since she'd probably never experience that kind of happiness again.

She had no idea what time it was when she sat down at her desk and began typing again. As soon as her fingers touched the keyboard, she didn't stop until she finished the last paragraph. She read and reread every line until her eyes blurred and her body screamed for sleep. The second she hit the Send button, she was certain that it was time to put an end to *The Quest* series for good.

Ironically, though, she'd finally done what she'd set out to do. She'd become just like her hero at a time when she desired to be anything but. She had found the courage she needed to lay her heart on the line and tell Sierra what she wanted. She stayed away from painkillers and anything else, even after the beating her body and heart had taken. She was finally the kind of woman worthy of Sierra, and Sierra was long gone.

❖

Sierra powered down her computer and grabbed her purse. Work was always slower during the fall months, allowing her more time to think, to remember. The days that had passed since the cruise had been filled with emptiness. It had been sixty-three days since the last time she'd seen Jaime. Time heals all? What a crock, she thought. The only thing time gave her was the ability to reflect. It allowed her to put her emotions aside and analyze the situation until she'd run out of alternative endings. Jaime had said she'd wanted a happy ending. Why couldn't she have been strong enough to give it to her?

Over the many weeks she questioned whether she'd made the right decision. She would have been a fool to make the same mistake twice. At least that's what she told her reflection every morning. But when it came to Jaime, she was a fool. That's what love did to people. It made them irrational. Her heart had been battling her better judgment ever since. Some days her rational side won small skirmishes, but somehow her instinct screamed that her heart would eventually win the war. A lot of good that did her now.

Her colleagues had been trying desperately to get her to date, figuring it was the best way to get her back out into the real world.

She'd even agreed to a blind date Friday—a good-friend-of-a-friend sort of thing. Dinner and a little conversation. That she could do. But no way could she imagine anyone but Jaime touching her. Even though they weren't together anymore, it seemed wrong, for some reason, and it was hard to imagine that she'd ever have that physical and emotional connection with anyone again.

Life wasn't fun anymore. Work had turned into a chore. Since returning, she hadn't worked more than four hours on any given day. Of course her boss was a total sweetie about the whole thing and told her she could take as much time as she needed. Today, she would expand on his offer and take a three-month sabbatical from everything—much-needed time to figure out what she really wanted out of life.

She didn't want to go home right away because returning to the emptiness of her apartment made her feel worse than she already did. She needed to be around people, but not around nosy, questioning people. Since that left most of her friends and colleagues out, she opted for a coffee and a pumpkin scone, at a corner café not too far from her home.

Holding back the tears that threatened to fall was difficult, especially since a cute elderly couple was sitting next to her fawning all over each other. The hand-holding and the sweet looks they gave one another reminded her that Jaime had asked her for that type of relationship. But the pureness of two people utterly in love completely gutted her. Similar scenes had never bothered her before, until now. Until Jaime. She looked away when the couple leaned toward each other for a kiss, not understanding why anyone didn't recognize her pain. Watching others enjoy their lives when she was so miserable was sadistic. Of course she had no one to blame but herself.

Times like these reminded her of their last night on the ship. Jaime had bared her soul and what had she done? She'd stomped all over Jaime's heart and refused to separate Jaime from injustices in her own past. She'd had plenty of time since to discern that Jaime and Eric were nothing alike. Eric had been so rough, so caveman-like. When he didn't get what he wanted he pouted. If that didn't work, he resorted to anger. The drinking magnified his dark moods. He'd pound his fist, raise his voice. In the end he used those fists on her.

Jaime had done none of that. She'd always spoken sweetly to her in loving tones. Her touch had always been gentle. Her eyes had burned so brightly they'd warmed Sierra's skin. But the most important thing she'd discovered during their time apart was that Jaime had never really lied to her. No matter how much it pained Jaime to tell her about her past, she'd still found the courage to do so, after only a few days. She took responsibility for her shortcomings and asked forgiveness for her sins. That alone should have proved to her that Jaime was nothing like Eric. She'd turned into a handsome, remarkable woman. Her fans had seen that. Her friend Darlene knew it. Too bad she couldn't have opened her eyes long enough to see it too before she'd decided to punish Jaime instead of taking responsibility for her own misgivings.

Unable to stomach any more of the sappy scene coming from the other table, she decided to leave when she recognized a familiar person standing in line at the coffee bar. She nearly jumped out of her chair when the woman turned to look at her with an angry expression. Darlene bolted out the door, Sierra not far behind.

"Darlene, hold up!"

She caught up with Darlene and grabbed her by the arm, swinging Darlene around to face her. The look Darlene threw her was deadly.

"What do you want?" Darlene said, pulling away.

"I…well…" Good question. What did she want? She didn't stop to think long enough to ponder that. She'd just reacted when she saw Darlene, glad for the instant connection to Jaime through her. What did that mean?

"Look, honestly, I don't give a *fuck* what you want. I gotta go."

"No! Stop. Please." This was the closest she'd been to Jaime in months. She'd always be a little jealous of their friendship, but she could live with that. However, she couldn't allow Darlene to walk away. Not yet. Not without knowing how Jaime was doing.

"Jesus," Darlene said. "You look worse than she sounds."

"She? You mean Jaime?"

"Who the hell else do you think I mean? Of course, Jaime."

"Is she okay? Hurt?" *Oh, God, she can't be hurt. I'm not there for her. What if she's suffering?*

"No, she's fine. She healed well after the Tyson incident."

"I'm sorry? Tyson incident?" What was Darlene talking about? "I don't understand."

"Oh, yeah. I forgot. You'd already bailed on her that night."

"Jesus, Darlene. Tell me already." She shook Darlene's arm in a panic.

"Bo beat her up the last night on the ship. Cracked a few ribs, busted up one side of her face. I thought you knew."

"Oh, God!" Of course she didn't know. She'd left early the next morning, making sure she was the first one off the ship so she wouldn't run into Jaime. "But you said she's fine."

"Yeah. At least I *think* she is. I haven't seen her since we returned, and except for short conversations by phone she doesn't talk to me. She won't see anyone since you dismissed her like a bad dream."

Darlene couldn't have said anything worse. Jaime had shut herself away again and this time it was all her fault. "Darlene, you have to make her see you. Don't let her hide."

"You just don't get it, do you?" Darlene said in obvious annoyance. "It's not my choice. It's hers. Unlike you, I respect her decisions. Besides," Darlene said, her jaw tightening, "she blames me."

"Why? This is all my fault, not yours. Maybe if I talk to her—"

"Oh, hell no. You've done enough. Now get outta my way." Darlene pushed past her and made it to the end of the block before Sierra used her body as a poor form of a barrier. "Sierra, get out of my way. You'll lose. Trust me."

"Too late," she said, wiping a tear away with the back of her hand. "I've already lost. Nothing you could do or say to me could make me feel any worse than I already do."

"Really?" Darlene crossed her arms over her chest. "Let's test that theory. It's my fault because I talked her into going on the cruise in the first place. I hoped you would be there. I knew if I could get you two to repair your friendship it would help her in her recovery. Honestly, I didn't think your relationship would progress as fast as it did, but for the first time in a long while, she was happy and I was happy for her. She's been alone for so long. All those women in the past never meant anything to her. Then you waltzed right back into her life, only to march right back out of it. I begged Jaime to tell you from the start but she was scared."

"That's what I don't get," she said. "She told me the same thing, but she knows she could always tell me anything."

"Bullshit!" Darlene said, her mouth a hard line. "And what happened when you found out?"

"I…" *I pushed her away. Couldn't accept who she was.*

"Exactly."

"But, Darlene, you don't understand. It was hard for me too. I didn't want to leave."

"You didn't have to," Darlene said. "Besides, you're too selfish for that. No, it was so much worse. She told me. She walked away from you. I'm guessing that was the hardest thing she's ever had to do."

Okay, so she'd been wrong. She thought she'd felt bad before, but the sting of Darlene's words felt like a needle piercing her heart. She held her hands tight over her chest, as if her heart would somehow stop beating if she let go. "You don't think she'd do anything stupid, do you?"

Darlene straightened, her eyes narrowing. "Like what, Sierra? You mean drink? Take something? She hasn't touched anything in over a year and a half, and I'm quite sure she's not doing any of that now."

"You say that," she said, as doubt clouded her better judgment. "But you said it yourself, you haven't seen her."

"I don't have to see Jaime to know what she's doing because, unlike you, I'm actually her friend. I believe in her. I know who she is, inside and out, which is more than I can say for you."

Darlene disappeared around the corner, leaving her to chew on her words. Darlene was right—about all of it. She was selfish.

Not only had Jaime not lied, Sierra had been the one to lie to Jaime. She'd promised she'd always be there for her, and then when times got tough, she allowed her fears to get the best of her and she'd pushed Jaime away. Maybe she hadn't run this time, but she'd done something far worse. She'd let go.

❖

Jaime plopped her feet onto the coffee table and cradled the receiver between her shoulder and ear. For the past half hour, she'd been discussing her decision to end *The Quest* series with her editor, who apparently wasn't happy with the conclusion of the current book. This was their third conversation in the past week, because her editor, if nothing else, was persistent.

"Jaime, are you sure before we release this tomorrow? I'll pull the plug, make some excuse." Margo was almost pleading.

"Positive, Margo. It ends this way. After this one, I'm done."

"How can you say that? You're so talented. There's still so much room for growth within these stories. Not to mention the other ideas I know you have within you. I don't understand what's changed, but I do know what you're capable of and it's so much more. Promise me you'll think about this?"

She closed her eyes and sighed. No more promises. They were too easily broken. "I don't need to think about anything. You've got the manuscript. Do what you need to do with it. Once this book is released, I'm planning on an extended vacation."

"Where are you going? It's the fucking middle of winter, and I know for a fact that snow ain't your thing."

"An editor using the word 'ain't.' I'm surprised you haven't been struck by lightning."

"Smart-ass. And you didn't answer my question."

"I don't know," she said quietly. "Anywhere but here."

"Jaime," Margo said, her tone softer. "Are you sure this is what you want?"

"I'm not sure of anything anymore."

CHAPTER TWENTY

Sierra looked across the table at her date, wondering how she'd gotten herself into this situation. She should have told her meddling friend that it was too soon to date, but here she was having a conversation about the perfect red wine, wishing she was home in bed wrapped around a good book.

In most circles, Brayden Jorgensen would have been considered the perfect catch. Tall, thick-shouldered with a slim waist, she oozed sex appeal. Her eyes were the color of milk chocolate and her lip curled upward just enough when she smiled that Sierra couldn't help but smile back. Brayden was arresting, but she still wasn't Jaime.

"How's the chicken piccata?" Brayden asked between sips of wine.

"Good, actually. Little strong on the garlic but otherwise cooked perfectly." She hoped that her subtle hint indicated to Brayden that there would be no makeout sessions later that evening. Brayden's light nod and the purse of those full lips meant she had made her point effectively.

"I know we don't know each other well," Brayden said, cutting into her filet. "But may I ask you a personal question?"

Try not at all. "Go ahead."

"You seem...how should I say this tactfully...distracted. I'm a great listener if you need an ear."

"Trust me. You don't want to hear about my problems."

"Why don't I be the judge of that?"

Well, this was just peachy. Was she really contemplating talking to her date about the person she was in love with? Sure, she'd been out of the dating scene for a while, but there had to be some dating-for-dummies advice of the top-ten no-no's of what not to discuss on the first date. Former lovers you were still in love with had to rank in the top two. "I wouldn't even know where to start."

"Simple," Brayden said. "Let's start with her name."

"Excuse me?" She stared at Brayden.

"I've had some experience with that pained expression you've been sporting all evening. If you don't want to talk about it—"

"Jaime. Her name is Jaime." Wow, amazing how something as simple as saying Jaime's name out loud made her feel better.

"How long have you two been apart?"

"What are you, some kind of mind reader?" *Please say yes because I don't want to be that easy to read.* "I apologize. That was rude of me."

"No, you're fine." Brayden smiled. "And no, I'm not, but I don't need to be a mind reader to know when another woman's heart is broken. I know the signs and you, my beautiful Sierra, are a roadmap of heartbreak."

"Did someone break your heart, Brayden?"

"Yes. But that's another story. Tell me about this Jaime person."

She talked for the next half hour as Brayden sat back, apparently content to just listen. Brayden nodded at the appropriate times and didn't offer advice or pry about personal details. Two glasses of wine later, she'd pretty much told Brayden the entire story.

"I'm sorry about this," Sierra said. "Bad first-date conversation."

"But good company," Brayden said. "I actually enjoy stimulating conversation. You'd be surprised how many dates I've been on lately where the conversation was lacking."

"I'm glad I can be so accommodating then. But seriously, this has to be pretty awkward for you."

"Under most circumstances I'd agree. Really, Sierra, I'm enjoying the evening. I am intrigued though. If you're still in love with Jaime, why did you allow her to walk away?"

"Because I couldn't handle it. The pressure and everything. The possibility of ending up in the same situation I was in before, you know?"

"Does she live close by?"

"I don't know," she said, toying with her wine glass. "We never exchanged numbers. She's a famous author though. Writes lesbian romances."

"Whoa! You don't mean Jaime Rivers, do you?"

"Yeah," she said, surprised. "Do you know her?"

"No, but I know *of* her. Who doesn't?" It wasn't a question. "She writes the Flynn Russell series. They're incredible. So much action and adventure. I never want to put one down once I start. In fact, a new one just came out the other day. Have you read it yet?"

"No." She tried to catch her breath. Jaime had finished it. She was so proud of her.

"That's too bad. It's stirring up a lot of controversy. I've been meaning to pick up a copy to see what all the hype's about but haven't found the time." The waitress returned and placed the check on the table. Brayden scooped it up before she could grab it. "Uh-uh. My treat."

"Thank you, Brayden. That's very sweet."

"You're most welcome."

The waitress scurried off as Brayden helped her into her coat and offered her arm before walking her to her car. Brayden's gallantry and striking good looks would make her the perfect mate for some lucky girl one day. But Sierra wanted Jaime.

"I'm really sorry about this," Sierra said, kissing Brayden on the cheek.

"Not a problem. As I said, I had a nice evening regardless. You have my number. Call if anything should change. Good night."

Brayden climbed into her Jag and the beautiful silver bullet raced off into the night. Sierra wondered what kind of foolish woman could have broken Brayden's heart and would have pondered that question further if she didn't need to be somewhere else.

❖

Sierra stared at the cover of Jaime's recent release, her hands trembling. She was scared to touch the book, afraid it could somehow scorch her skin. She knew what would happen as soon as she opened it. Every line she read would bring back memories of Jaime in her arms. Those were Jaime's words on those pages, her thoughts, her creativity that had brought Flynn to life. It didn't matter that they told a story about a fictional character. Jaime was responsible for them and it was the closest Sierra would have been to her in months.

Nothing she'd done since the cruise could wipe Jaime from her mind. She could still feel Jaime's skin against hers. She missed the way Jaime trembled when she came in her arms. Sometimes she could swear she tasted Jaime on her fingertips—that delicious sweat-soaked-skin flavor after they'd made love. Those thoughts were forever etched in her mind, the only thing that kept her connected to Jaime, until that damn book.

Since returning she'd read all the other Flynn novels, but she'd heard this one was different. She'd Googled a few reviews before arriving at the bookstore, and the critics weren't happy. They'd said they didn't like its ending, thought Flynn deserved better. She had no idea what they were talking about and wouldn't until she read it herself.

The book sat erect in its stand, taunting her like a lover spread naked before her. She could hear it calling out to her, beckoning her to pick it up and hold it like a precious treasure in her hands. The first touch of its glossy cover brought back images of Jaime's skin sliding under her fingertips. They tingled with every caress, every touch. She closed her eyes. One touch. She'd sell her soul for just one more touch.

She flipped the book over and stared at the back cover, running one finger over Jaime's picture. Amazing how that smile could still hold her captive. She missed everything about Jaime, from her cocky grin to her hearty laugh when they teased each other. But what she missed most was staring into Jaime's fathomless green eyes, watching them churn with her rising passion while Sierra made love to her. The way Jaime tensed then shattered as Sierra brought her to orgasm, how Jaime cried out her name when she took

Jaime between her lips. These memories, like all the rest, brought a flood of desire coursing between her legs. She grabbed the counter for support, thankful no one was watching.

Finding the strength to move again, she paid for the book and drove home in silence. No radio. Nothing to distract her from thoughts of Jaime. She snuggled in front of the fireplace, holding Jaime's book close to her heart. Breathing deeply before daring to open it, she was almost afraid to begin what the bookstore clerk called Flynn's final journey.

A few pages in, she gasped and hot salty tears fell down her face and onto the page. It was all she could do to breathe.

S,

This book is dedicated to the only woman I ever loved. I'm sorry that I couldn't be your real-life hero, but hopefully, through my story, you will see everything I wanted to be for you and more.

J

Flynn's story unfolded page after page, and Sierra stayed put on the couch until she reached the end. She could feel Jaime's pain in every word. Flynn had suffered not because of Alex but because of her own mistakes. Suddenly, her anger bubbled to the surface. Flynn didn't deserve this ending and neither did Jaime's fans. She reread the last paragraph, the feeling of loss echoing loudly in her ears.

Flynn looked out over the horizon, seeing no beauty in the kaleidoscope of colors. She hadn't witnessed beauty in months and wondered if she ever would again.

She'd spent every moment for the last year searching for Alex with no luck. She'd even resorted to using some of her contacts, but nobody would tell her anything about Alex's mysterious whereabouts.

Waking up every morning without Alex by her side left her with a void no other could fill. The pain had dulled the light in her eyes and was the reason Flynn no longer thirsted for adventure. Her hunger for the unknown was no longer driving her. She had quit her job with the agency. She vowed she would spend the rest of her life looking for the one person who meant everything to her, even if she always remained just beyond her reach. Alex had to be out there somewhere and Flynn would not rest until she found her.

She set the book down and closed her eyes, allowing the tears to fall. Flynn wasn't the only one willing to search out her lover. Moving to her computer, she began to Google everything available about Jaime. After hours of searching she'd found what she'd been looking for. The time had come for a new chapter in both their lives. She picked up her keys and headed out to find the one person who could guarantee her a happy ending.

CHAPTER TWENTY-ONE

Jaime watched the rain fall steadily from the menacing storm clouds in the morning sky. The clouds matched her dark, ominous mood. She should have stayed in bed, but after receiving her editor's phone call, she couldn't resist the temptation to log onto her fan page. Her book had sparked a lot of controversy in the last few days, most of it negative.

The second the final book in the Flynn Russell series hit the shelves it climbed to the top of the charts. Within the first few days, the fans began to question its ending. It pained her to admit that her editor was right. Her Web site and Fan Blog went crazy. People couldn't believe Jaime had ended the series in quite that fashion, and to be honest, until she wrote the final lines, it had even surprised her.

Fans of her book lashed out immediately. "It was too painful," one wrote. Another said, "Flynn deserved better." Others chastised Jaime's judgment. "What were you thinking?" a fan posted on her blog. "How could you be so insensitive to Flynn after everything she's done for you?"

The last comment made Jaime laugh. Wasn't she the writer? Wasn't Flynn her character? Didn't she give Flynn life—make people believe she was real flesh and blood? She was the one with the power to decide Flynn's fate. Maybe she didn't do Flynn's character justice, but that had been her decision. She was the one who'd have to live with it.

And she had other things on her mind. Sierra was constantly in her thoughts, constantly pushing through the barriers that she had erected when she returned home. Walking through that door haunted her every day. If she were only stronger maybe she could have fought more—made Sierra listen to her. But she knew why she didn't. One look at the pain and disappointment on Sierra's face meant Sierra's feelings had changed for her. Nothing she could have said would have altered Sierra's mind. She could finally accept that, but it wasn't easy.

She thought that going through the withdrawal process was hard, but it was nothing compared to having Sierra ripped from her life. After experiencing making love with Sierra—becoming intoxicated with her smell, her smile, her laugh—Sierra had turned out to be her new addiction. And when she couldn't have her any longer, the withdrawal process was more physically and emotionally painful than any substance could elicit.

When the pain of loneliness became too great, Jaime had inevitably allowed Darlene to visit. Darlene had rushed over when she called, throwing her arms around her neck to hug her before swatting her on the head. Darlene told her it was for shutting her out and warned her that she'd better never do that to her again. She'd laughed. She'd missed her.

She tried to explain to Darlene how she felt, how every day since walking away from Sierra was more painful than the last. Every breath of air burned her throat. Every drink of water did nothing to quench her thirst. She was lost and alone—her cross to carry for her sins. Darlene, being her usual self, told her to stop being so damned dramatic. But hey, she couldn't completely change herself over overnight.

Her life had changed, though, and hopefully she'd become a stronger person in the end. Since Sierra, she'd found the courage to stand up for something she wanted even though she'd lost it. She'd finished her book, no matter how hard it was to write down the words. In the last few days, she'd even stopped hiding and had actually made a conscious effort to leave the house. Last night she'd met one of their former classmates for dinner who had reached out to her on Facebook. That was progress, right?

One day at a time. One day at a time.

The sound of the doorbell startled her, making her trip over the suitcases in the doorway. Who the hell was at her door at eight on a Sunday morning? She wanted to ignore the insistent pounding but couldn't ignore the urgency in the knock. When she yanked the door open, she nearly stumbled backward from the shock.

"You've been injured in a shark attack. You have some issues, but hey, who doesn't? You are the most incredible woman I've ever met. And I'd be stupid to ignore that. Anything I missed?"

"Wh…what?"

Sierra moved through the doorway, closing the door behind her. "I *asked* if there was anything else? Because before I throw myself at your feet and beg you to take me back, I want to know everything there is to know about you, Jaime Rivers."

She steadied herself against the wall with one hand as she reached out to touch Sierra with the other. She had to know if she was real. Sierra, with her hair fanned out around her face, no makeup, and looking like she hadn't slept in weeks, was too beautiful to be a dream. "What are you doing here?"

"I'm here because I need you," Sierra said, cradling Jaime's hand and kissing her palm. "Because you're all I think about." She wrapped her arms around Jaime's neck. "And because I love you and refuse to live another day without you." She kissed Jaime softly, conveying with that one touch that everything she was saying was true. "I should have told you on that ship. I've loved you since the first day we met, and I will love you until my very last breath. I'm sorry I've been so stupid."

"You should have been the writer," Jaime whispered, her heart beating steadily for the first time in months.

"Oh, why's that?"

"Because that was the most poetic thing I've ever heard." She buried her face in Sierra's hair, allowing the tears to fall.

"Oh, baby. Don't cry."

"Can't help it."

They held each other for a long time, sharing tears and kisses of joy. Neither one moved. Neither one wanted to.

"How the hell did you find me?" She pulled back a little but refused to allow Sierra out from the circle of her arms.

"Google. And let me tell you it wasn't easy. I'll explain all about that later. Right now I want to say I'm sorry. I should have thought things through. I overreacted. Please, can you forgive—"

She stopped Sierra's rambling with a kiss. She had gone too long without the simple pleasure and refused to wait any longer. When she released Sierra they were both breathless. "I love you too. And I don't want you to apologize. The blame's mine. I should have told you everything the moment we became friends again. I just never wanted to disappoint you."

"You've never disappointed me—ever! You've always been the one who was there for me no matter what. And what did I do to you the moment I found out something that upset me? I pushed you away. I'm sorry. I'm so damn sorry."

She pulled Sierra close, erasing the small distance between them. Having Sierra there in her arms gave her hope, but she had to say a few things if they had any chance at all of a future together. The one thing she'd learned after their separation was that she was done apologizing for who she was. "I'm sorry too. But I'm not perfect, Sierra. Now you know who I am, what I've become, what if I let you down again? What if there's something else about me that you don't like or can't live with? Are you going to walk away again?"

"Baby, stop." Sierra put her finger over Jaime's lips. "There's *nothing* about you that I don't love. I know you, in here," she said placing Jaime's hand over her heart. "You're my hero, Jaime. You always will be. I was an idiot to let my fear keep us apart."

She closed her eyes and placed her head against Sierra's forehead. She so desperately wanted to believe those words, but fear still warred with doubt. "If that's true, then you have to promise me one more thing or this isn't going to work."

"Anything," Sierra whispered.

"Promise me forever."

"How about I show you instead?"

She guided Sierra to her bedroom, where they undressed each other slowly with the knowledge this time that they had the rest of their lives to love and be loved by one other. Once she lowered Sierra to the bed, she planted soft, tender kisses over every inch of Sierra's bare skin. When Sierra bowed beneath her and begged for her touch, she slid her hand between Sierra's legs with the intent of touching her soul.

"I love you inside me, baby," Sierra said, opening her legs wider for Jaime to slide between them.

"I love touching you. I love you." The moment Jaime's lips encircled Sierra's clitoris, Sierra cried out. She pumped her hips in time with Jaime's firm strokes as the orgasm raced along her spine. When the tremors receded, Jaime crawled up her body and cradled her, her head resting on Jaime's shoulder. It felt so, so right.

"You're amazing," she said, as she lay limp and sated in Jaime's arms. "I love you."

"I love you too." She pulled Sierra closer, if that was possible.

They kissed once again, whispering words of devotion to each other. Moments passed, and when they finally broke apart, she raised herself on an elbow. "Can I ask you a question?" Jaime nodded. "I couldn't help but notice the suitcases in your hallway. Are you going somewhere?"

"Yeah," Jaime admitted reluctantly. "I planned to take a sabbatical from everything. You know, to gain a new perspective on things." She groaned when Sierra ran a finger over her stomach and her muscles tightened.

"You mean you were running away."

She saw no use in denying the obvious. She hadn't been able to bear the thought of living without Sierra. Luckily, after today, her future looked brighter. "You're right, in a way. I couldn't figure out how to live without you so I wanted something new. But I'm thinking, after recent events, that maybe we can both see it as a change for the better."

"I like the sound of that. But what about Flynn?"

She looked at Sierra, surprised. "I didn't realize you were a fan."

"Your biggest. And don't you forget it," Sierra said, poking her in the ribs. "Now tell me why Alex left Flynn."

"Simple. It was time."

"I don't believe that and neither do you. Flynn is an amazing character. She's passionate, bold. She has more adventures left in her, baby. I think all your readers know that too."

"Funny, that's what my editor said."

"And maybe you should have listened to her, honey. It's not too late. Write another book. Finish her story."

She brought her lips to Sierra's, groaning when Sierra pulled away. "Sierra—"

"I will not let you skirt this issue, Jaime. No kissing until we talk this out, because I can't think when you do that. And when I start kissing you again, I don't plan to stop."

"I don't know if I can," Jaime whispered. "What if her story really is over?"

"Sure, you can do it. You're Jaime Rivers. You're my hero. You can do anything."

She closed her eyes, hoping Sierra wouldn't be mad at her for what she was about to confess. "I ended it that way because I didn't get the girl in the end. For once, I became Flynn at a time when I was anything but a hero."

"Oh, baby." Sierra kissed her cheeks. "I didn't mean to hurt you. You have to believe me. I could hear the sadness in every word you wrote. I'm so sorry I put you through that."

"*You* didn't put me through anything. Do you think I blame you? Because I don't. It's true I relate to Flynn in some ways, but in others we are so very different. *I* should have been bolder, fought harder for you. I gave up too easily, and I'm sorry for that. I was a coward."

"Now you listen to me," Sierra said, sitting up and straddling Jaime. She pinned Jaime's hands above her head and stared intently at her. "You will never say that again, do you hear?"

"But it's true, Sierra, and I swear it will never happen again. I can see now that Alex's leaving may have hurt Flynn, but at least she finally experienced love, even if it was only for a little while."

"Darling, that's depressing."

"Yeah, it is." Jaime grinned. "But I'm thinking it may make for a great fifth book."

The sparkle in Jaime's eyes told Sierra she wasn't kidding. "Really! You're going to write another one?"

"You betcha. I'm thinking Flynn has one more adventure left in her. Besides, something seems to have sparked my imagination all of a sudden. Maybe you can *motivate* me?"

"How's this for motivation?" She trailed kisses down Jaime's neck, causing her lover to shiver.

"You definitely inspire me."

"And what about Flynn?"

Jaime grabbed Sierra's hand and placed it between her legs. "Let's just say she has a certain someone to find, and when this next adventure is over, she'll never want for anything else again."

"Sounds like you'll both get your happy ending."

"Looks like we all will."

About the Author

L.T. Marie is a career athlete who writes during her free time. Her hobbies are reading every lesbian romance she can get her hands on, working out, and watching Giants baseball. Her first novel, *Three Days*, was published in October 2011.

Books Available From Bold Strokes Books

Ladyfish by Andrea Bramhall. Finn's escape to the Florida Keys leads her straight into the arms of scuba diving instructor Oz as she fights for her freedom, their blossoming love...and her life! (978-1-60282-747-9)

Spanish Heart by Rachel Spangler. While on a mission to find herself in Spain, Ren Molson runs the risk of losing her heart to her tour guide, Lina Montero. (978-1-60282-748-6)

Love Match by Ali Vali. When Parker "Kong" King, the number one tennis player in the world, meets commercial pilot Captain Sydney Parish, sparks fly but not from attraction. They have the summer to see if they have a love match. (978-1-60282-749-3)

One Touch by L.T. Marie. A romance writer and a travel agent come together at their high school reunion, only to find out that the memory of that one touch never fades. (978-1-60282-750-9)

Night Shadows: Queer Horror edited by Greg Herren and J.M. Redmann. *Night Shadows* features delightfully wicked stories by some of the biggest names in queer publishing. (978-1-60282-751-6)

Secret Societies by William Holden. An outcast hustler, his unlikely "mother," his faithless lovers, and his religious persecutors—all in 1726. (978-1-60282-752-3)

The Raid by Lee Lynch. Before Stonewall, having a drink with friends or your girl could mean jail. Would these women and men still have family, a job, a place to live after...The Raid. (978-1-60282-753-0)

The You Know Who Girls by Annameekee Hesik. As they begin freshman year, Abbey Brooks and her best friend, Kate, pinky swear they'll keep away from the lesbians in Gila High, but Abbey already suspects she's one of those you-know-who girls herself and slowly learns who her true friends really are. (978-1-60282-754-7)

Wyatt: Doc Holliday's Account of an Intimate Friendship by Dale Chase. Erotica writer Dale Chase takes the remarkable friendship between Wyatt Earp, upright lawman, and Doc Holliday, southern gentlemen turned gambler and killer, to an entirely new level: hot! (978-1-60282-755-4)

Month of Sundays by Yolanda Wallace. Love doesn't always happen overnight; sometimes it takes a month of Sundays. (978-1-60282-739-4)

Jacob's War by C.P. Rowlands. ATF Special Agent Allison Jacob's task force is in the middle of an all-out war, from the streets to the boardrooms of America. Small business owner Katie Blackburn is the latest victim who accidentally breaks it wide open but may break AJ's heart at the same time. (978-1-60282-740-0)

The Pyramid Waltz by Barbara Ann Wright. Princess Katya Nar Umbriel wants a perfect romance, but her Fiendish nature and duties to the crown mean she can never tell the truth-until she meets Starbride, a woman who gets to the heart of every secret, even if it will be the death of her. (978-1-60282-741-7)

The Secret of Othello by Sam Cameron. Florida teen detectives Steven and Denny risk their lives to search for a sunken NASA satellite—but under the waves, no one can hear you scream… (978-1-60282-742-4)

Dreaming of Her by Maggie Morton. Isa has begun to dream of the most amazing woman—a woman named Lilith with a gorgeous face, an amazing body, and the ability to turn Isa on like no other. But Lilith is just a dream…isn't she? (978-1-60282-847-6)

Andy Squared by Jennifer Lavoie. Andrew never thought anyone could come between him and his twin sister, Andrea...until Ryder rode into town. (978-1-60282-743-1)

Finding Bluefield by Elan Barnehama. Set in the backdrop of Virginia and New York and spanning the years 1960-1982, Finding Bluefield chronicles the lives of Nicky Stewart, Barbara Philips, and their son, Paul, as they struggle to define themselves as a family. (978-1-60282-744-8)

The Jetsetters by David-Matthew Barnes. As rock band The Jetsetters skyrocket from obscurity to super stardom, Justin Holt, a lonely barista, and Diego Delgado, the band's guitarist, fight with everything they have to stay together, despite the chaos and fame. (978-1-60282-745-5)

Strange Bedfellows by Rob Byrnes. Partners in life and crime, Grant Lambert and Chase LaMarca, are hired to make a politician's compromising photo disappear, but what should be an easy job quickly spins out of control. (978-1-60282-746-2)

Speed Demons by Gun Brooke. When NASCAR star Evangeline Marshall returns to the race track after a close brush with death, will famous photographer Blythe Pierce document her triumph and reciprocate her love—or will they succumb to their respective demons and fail? (978-1-60282-678-6)

Summoning Shadows: A Rosso Lussuria Vampire Novel by Winter Pennington. The Rosso Lussuria vampires face enemies both old and new, and to prevail they must call on even more strange alliances, unite as a clan, and draw on every weapon within their reach—but with a clan of vampires, that's easier said than done. (978-1-60282-679-3)

Sometime Yesterday by Yvonne Heidt. When Natalie Chambers learns her Victorian house is haunted by a pair of lovers and a Dark Man, can she and her lover Van Easton solve the mystery that will set the ghosts free and banish the evil presence in the house? Or will they have to run to survive as well? (978-1-60282-680-9)

Into the Flames by Mel Bossa. In order to save one of his patients, psychiatrist Jamie Scarborough will have to confront his own monsters—including those he unknowingly helped create. (978-1-60282-681-6)

Coming Attractions: Author's Edition by Bobbi Marolt. For Helen Townsend, chasing turns to caring, and caring turns to loving, but will love take five steps back and turn to leaving? (978-1-60282-732-5)

OMGqueer, edited by Radclyffe and Katherine E. Lynch. Through stories imagined and told by youth across America, this anthology provides a snapshot of queerness at the dawn of the new millennium. (978-1-60282-682-3)

Oath of Honor by Radclyffe. A First Responders novel. First do no harm…First Physician of the United States Wes Masters discovers that being the president's doctor demands more than brains and personal sacrifice—especially when politics is the order of the day. (978-1-60282-671-7)

A Question of Ghosts by Cate Culpepper. Becca Healy hopes Dr. Joanne Call can help her learn if her mother really committed suicide—but she's not sure she can handle her mother's ghost, a decades-old mystery, and lusting after the difficult Dr. Call without some serious chocolate consumption. (978-1-60282-672-4)

The Night Off by Meghan O'Brien. When Emily Parker pays for a taboo role-playing fantasy encounter from the Xtreme Encounters escort agency, she expects to surrender control—but never imagines losing her heart to dangerous butch Nat Swayne. (978-1-60282-673-1)

Sara by Greg Herren. A mysterious and beautiful new student at Southern Heights High School stirs things up when students start dying. (978-1-60282-674-8)

Fontana by Joshua Martino. Fame, obsession, and vengeance collide in a novel that asks: What if America's greatest hero was gay? (978-1-60282-675-5)

Lemon Reef by Robin Silverman. What would you risk for the memory of your first love? When Jenna Ross learns her high school love Del Soto died on Lemon Reef, she refuses to accept the medical examiner's report of a death from natural causes and risks everything to find the truth. (978-1-60282-676-2)

The Dirty Diner: Gay Erotica on the Menu, edited by Jerry L. Wheeler. Gay erotica set in restaurants, featuring food, sex, and men—could you really ask for anything more? (978-1-60282-677-9)

Sweat: Gay Jock Erotica by Todd Gregory. Sizzling tales of smoking hot sex with the athletic studs everyone fantasizes about. (978-1-60282-669-4)